To Brandon
John L. Hough

The Young American Series
Book 2

Spirit of the Buffalo

By
John L. Hough

Renegade Publishing
P.O. Box 544
Camp Verde, AZ 86322

www.RenegadePublishing.com

Cover Art by **Betty Ramirez-Atkins**
32281 Hwy 160
Cortez, CO 81321
FAX 970-565-2339

Taken from Original Oil Painting by **Twyla Hough**

NON STRIPABLE COVER

THE YOUNG AMERICAN SERIES
BOOK 2
SPIRIT OF THE BUFFALO
PUBLISHED BY

Renegade Publishing
P.O. Box 544
Camp Verde, AZ 86322

www.RenegadePublishing.com

Copyright 2000 by John L. Hough
Printed in the United States of America
Library of Congress Card Number: 00-191941
ISBN-0-97404050-2-2

Chapter One

"I will be careful ma, trust me," Jeremy found himself saying for the tenth time that morning. They had gone over it so many times that he was becoming more than a little irritated at his mother's constant worrying. Since the very moment that his parents had agreed to let him go spend the winter with his adopted Cheyenne family, she had become more and more apprehensive, coming up with one excuse after another why he shouldn't go. Only the argument of spending time with his relatives had finally convinced her, and that had been a flimsy argument at best.

He and his blood brother, Runs with the Wind, had done everything possible to calm her fears by describing how quiet and peaceful a snowed in Cheyenne winter camp was. Though he knew very little about it himself, Runs with the Wind had coached him well on precisely what points to bring up. He assured her that the two of them would be spending long days and nights in the lodge of his adopted father, Night Hawk, learning the ways of the spirits and the medicine man. Surely there would be no trouble for them to get into, even if they tried.

Cheryl raised her hand and opened her mouth to call out to her son one more time, as the two boys rode away from the cabin through the slowly falling snow. The valley floor was almost totally white, surrounded on all sides by the dark green of the pine trees. All the crops had been harvested, and enough wild grass had been cut and put up to get the horses through the winter. There were several cords of wood stacked in the lean-to, and there was plenty of dried and canned meat in the root cellar to get them through the winter, so even she couldn't put her finger on what it was that made her so unwilling to let him leave.

"Let him go dear," John said, placing a reassuring hand on his wife's shoulder. "He's in good hands, besides the snow will be to deep for them to get into any mischief before you know it."

Just then the two boys let out a wild war whoop and raced headlong down the valley to be swallowed up by the early winter storm.

A sudden shiver went down Cheryl's spine as a forbidding feeling overwhelmed her. Had she been able to reach her son at that moment, she would have snatched him out of the saddle and dragged him, kicking and screaming if necessary, back to the safety of the cabin. This was going to be a long winter, and even the warm smile on her husband's face couldn't wash away the apprehension she felt as she tried to get one last glimpse of her departing son.

Jeremy, on the other hand, felt nothing but sheer exhilaration as the wind whipped at his face and the tiny snowflakes stuck to his eyelashes making it hard to see. Every moment he spent with the Cheyenne people seemed to awaken the senses of his spirit, and stir up deeply buried emotions from beyond the reaches of his memory. Each story of the old days, that Night Hawk told so masterfully, could create such images in his head, that he felt he was actually a part of it. "Yes," Jeremy thought, "this is going to be anything but boring."

As they reached the end of the valley Runs with the Wind swung his horse off of the trail and headed south along a well used game trail.

"Hey, brother, I thought you said your camp was more to the east?"

"It is."

"Then why are we going south?"

"Because that's where the buffalo are, and you wouldn't want to miss the last big hunt of the season would you?"

"Why didn't you mention it before?"

"Do you think your mother and father would have let you come if they had known?"

"Probably not," Jeremy replied.

"This way your mother won't have something else to worry about."

"I guess you're right," Jeremy said, squirming slightly in his saddle as though he could feel his mother watching him.

"Well, are we going to sit here in the snow all day, or are we going to hunt buffalo?"

"We're going hunting of course, but are you sure we can catch the main hunting party?"

"We're going to get there first," Runs with the Wind said, beginning to lay out his plan. "The big herd is two days ride south of the village and the hunters will be moving slow so they don't spook the stragglers. We'll ride fast, staying to the west so we can get ahead of the buffalo and cut off their escape. We'll find a safe spot to set up an ambush where the buffalo will come right past us. With my bow and your rifle, and the buffalo so close, we should take many animals for our fathers lodge. Our people will be singing our praises all through the season of snow."

"What if we accidentally spook the buffalo first?"

"Then they run back toward the winter camp, and the main hunting party takes them by surprise closer to home. Either way, we can't lose."

"Seems like you got this all figured out," Jeremy said, sounding more convinced than he really was, "so what are we waiting for?"

On they rode, not realizing this was going to be the biggest test of their survival skills, and the toughest winter either one of them had ever faced.

The two boys turned their horses back to the south and kicked them up to a ground eating trot. They passed through the forest on an old trail that took them from the high mountain valley down a long ridge that led to the foot hills lining the western edge of the plains. By mid morning it was apparent that this was a typical early winter storm carrying only a little snow that wouldn't last through the day. Patches of blue sky were already showing and the sun was working desperately to burn off, or off, or push away the clouds that remained.

The boys rode on at a good pace, swiftly descending out of the high mountains where the heavier snow was falling. By the time the sun was nearly down the warm gentle breeze from the south had melted the last of the snow on the plains and all that remained was the dampness of the air and the ground to tell of its passing.

It was then, in the fading light of dusk that they saw the first small herd of about thirty buffalo on the edge of the prairie just below the sparsely wooded hills they were riding through.

"Is that them?" Jeremy asked, disappointed at how few animals were in the herd.

"No, that's just a bunch of stragglers that drifted away from the main herd. We'll see several small herds like that while we try to get ahead of them. Let's keep going, and be quiet so we don't spook them to early. If they run now, they will be going away from the village."

On they rode, through the fading light of dusk until they had gone a safe distance ahead so as not to cause any alarm among the buffalo. As the darkening sky made traveling over the wet broken ground almost impossible, Runs with the Wind turned his horse up a small canyon that led to the west. The scattered trees were thicker here, offering more cover and protection from the weather. After going a short distance he stopped and got down to hobble his horse's feet.

"We'll camp here so the breeze will carry our scent up the canyon and away from the buffalo."

Jeremy was putting hobbles on his horse also as he looked around for a dry place to sleep.

"The ground is still pretty wet," he said, thinking what a miserable night it was going to be.

"Over here brother, I see you still have much to learn. We'll sleep under that big cedar tree. See how the bottom limbs reach way out just above the ground? That'll mean the earth is dry underneath, and it's branches will protect us from the wind, and the morning frost."

"I suppose we can't have a fire either?"

"No, smoke makes buffalo think of prairie fires, and if the wind were to shift, even for a minute, the buffalo would panic. Tomorrow night we'll have a big fire, and all the roasted buffalo hump you can eat."

"I can't wait, but tonight we'll have to settle for the biscuits and fried chicken Ma sent with us. Hope you don't mind eating it cold."

"I don't mind eating your mothers cooking anytime."

"Yea, I noticed that at dinner last night. Just remember, half of this is mine."

After eating a cold meal they stretched out their blankets under the boughs of the giant cedar and drifted off into a restless sleep. Both boys dreamed of the success they would have in the coming hunt on the following day, and how proud everyone would be of the plan they had carried out so well to cut off the escaping buffalo.

It was going to be something alright. Jeremy could see the two of them now, returning to camp with the other hunters who were praising their skills, and the fact that the lion's share of the kill had been made by them. It was a well thought out plan, with two young hunters eagerly waiting to carry it out. What could possibly go wrong?

Chapter Two

It was a cold gray morning, with small flakes of snow already falling as Night Hawk emerged from his tepee to speak with Standing Bear. The chief of the Cheyenne had been waiting somewhat impatiently since waking the medicine man, but Night Hawk was in no hurry to get started. He yawned and breathed deeply of the brisk morning air as he stretched stiff sore muscles, that no longer rested as easy on the hard packed ground that was the floor of his lodge.

Thin gray wisps of smoke hung low over the frost covered lodges as a sense of excitement and anticipation filled the air. Even the camp dogs could feel it as they yipped and pulled at the rope tethers that held them in place so they couldn't run ahead and spoil the hunt. All indications for the coming event were favorable and the people were gathering at the south end of the camp preparing to leave.

"What do the spirits say?" Standing Bear asked as he looked out toward the plains that were becoming whiter all the time. He too knew the routine that Night Hawk was going through and the reluctance to leave the comfortable warm sleeping robes for an early morning trek across the plains. He was all to aware of how it felt because only a few minutes earlier he had been awakened by Spotted Horse and was also experiencing the stiff muscles that came with age, and the reluctance to start a new day. Neither man was old, but both had seen their prime come and go. It would be time for others to assume their responsibilities in less time than it would take a toddler to grow into a warrior. An eternity for a child, yet no time at all for a man who had seen many winter camps such as this one.

"They say we will be successful, but that we must move faster than we had planned. This shouldn't be a real winter snow today but it won't be long before it comes."

Night Hawk was pretty sure this wasn't going to be a heavy snow that would last, because the season was still early and the signs leading into real winter were not yet present. However all of this could change within a matter of two or three days, making it necessary to hurry along.

"The others are ready, and waiting only for you, and a blessing from the spirits," Standing Bear said, and as Night Hawk turned to lead his horse toward the waiting hunters he added, "Good hunting my friend."

As the hunters left camp, the female members of the hunting party followed on foot. They would reach the herd only after the men had finished their part. It would be the women's job to skin and butcher the meat while the hunters stood guard, alert for any danger that might happen by. But for now they would follow behind at a slower pace with an escort of four warriors who would leave them only when it was time to begin the hunt. By the time the main herd was located and plans had been decided on, the women would be close enough to be out of any real danger of being attacked by enemy bands hunting the same herd.

Standing Bear remained in the camp with a handful of his chosen warriors to protect the women and children, and the elders who couldn't make the trip. Theirs was the hardest job, one of waiting and not knowing. It was frustrating at times, but a necessary task to insure the survival of the people.

Night Hawk led the main party of hunters as they headed south. To the east and west were forward scouts that would warn them of any danger or small groups of buffalo that they might need to circle around.

On his right rode Antelope, the brother of his wife Quail,

and possibly one of the most skilled hunters in the entire Cheyenne nation. He was tall and lean and though no longer in his prime, he was still a long way from sitting in his lodge when there was hunting to be done. He was a patient and cautious hunter, but Antelope knew it was only Night Hawk's ability to communicate with the spirits that allowed him to read the thoughts of the buffalo, and know what they would do, even before they did. It was an enviable gift for any hunter and Antelope was happy just to hunt at his side.

On his left rode Spotted Horse, a young aggressive warrior that was stirring up quite a following of his peers. He put his heart and soul into every endeavor, no matter how small, and would accept nothing less than perfection to come from his efforts.

It was evident that Spotted Horse had his goal set on becoming the next Chief of the people, which wouldn't be so bad, if he could learn that war was a necessary evil at times, and not a hobby for young men with too much time on their hands.

Also apparent was his deep seated dislike, possibly even hatred of Night Hawk. Everyone knew that Spotted Horse blamed him, for the death of his younger brother, Little Feather. Night Hawk had done everything he could to dissuade the boy from going on a vision quest before he was ready, but Little Feather had insisted on proving to his brother that he was worthy to ride at his side. Now Spotted Horse was convinced that Night Hawk had called upon an evil panther spirit to punish the boy for going against his advice. For this Spotted Horse had silently vowed to get revenge. It wouldn't be easy, because for a Cheyenne to take the life of one of his own people would be unforgivable and cause him to be banished from the tribe. Yet he would get his revenge in a way that would place the blame on someone or something else. Many things could happen to a young warrior during battle or on a hunt such as this, and Runs with the Wind was a very young warrior. If something happened to him, it would crush the old Medicine Man, and Spotted Horse would have twice the revenge.

"It's to bad Runs with the Wind isn't here," he said to himself as they rode along.

"What?" Night Hawk asked, not certain he had heard correctly.

"I was saying it's to bad your son didn't get back in time

to join the hunt. I'm sure he wouldn't want to miss it."

"Yes, I thought he would be back by now, but there will be other hunts."

Both men fell back into the silence of riding along, but an eerie voice kept nagging in the back of Night Hawk's mind, "Why the sudden concern for my son. Spotted Horse has done everything he could in the past to make the boy look bad, and to forgive and forget, is not a part of his nature. I must speak to the Spirits on this as soon as the hunt is over."

Yet try as he might to concentrate on the task at hand, the sadistic grin on Spotted Horse's face kept coming back to interrupt the focus of his thoughts.

The hunting party traveled at a faster pace than they had originally planned, and by late afternoon when the sky began to clear, they had gone far enough to see some of the straggling buffalo off to the southwest. The hunting party started to swing to the east, hoping to pass by undetected. With a little luck they could surprise the herd early in the morning and be headed home by late afternoon, cutting a full day off of their trip.

"Little Wolf," Night Hawk called.

Within seconds the eager young warrior was at his side. Night Hawk was proud of the boy who was now hunting for the lodge of his old friend Gray Wolf. Since his father had been mauled by the great bear and could no longer hunt, Little Wolf had stepped up to fill his fathers moccasins, and Gray Wolf had never eaten better.

"Go back and tell the women to keep moving. When you join us at sunrise we will be ready."

"I'll be back before sunrise."

"No need to hurry, look over there."

Off to the west they could see the back end of the main herd. Little brown spots everywhere, getting thicker the farther west they looked, until the entire earth was darkened by their presence.

"Lead them right to this spot. We will be waiting."

Little Wolf wheeled his horse around and raced back across the plains the way he had come. Whether there was a need to hurry or not he wasn't taking any chances, there were more buffalo here than he had seen in his entire life, and this was one hunt he wasn't about to miss.

Chapter Three

The sun was starting to peek over the eastern horizon as Jeremy and Runs with the Wind crawled out from under the protective branches of the huge cedar tree that had sheltered them through the night. The sky was clear and crisp without a hint of wind in any direction. Renegade snorted and stomped the ground impatiently, anxious to be moving around in the cool morning air.

"You should teach him not to do that Jeremy."

"Teach him not to do what?"

"To snort and stomp. It tells everything, and everyone that you are near."

"I see what you mean," Jeremy said looking out the mouth of the canyon toward the prairie.

A small group of buffalo were standing only a few hundred yards away staring intently in their direction. They had heard something that didn't belong, but were unable to focus their poor eyesight well enough to identify the cause of the noise. The lead cow raised her head and sniffed the air cautiously, trying to locate the source of the sound. Unable to do so she took several steps toward the canyon and repeated the process. Still unable to detect any danger she returned to graze with the herd.

When Renegade started to raise his head to snort again, Jeremy clamped a hand over his nose. Holding his head down while patting him on the neck gave the horse the idea, and he was soon content to sniff the air and munch on the tender grass at his feet.

"Shouldn't we get going ?" Jeremy asked almost as eager to be on the way as Renegade.

"Soon, the plan was to hit the main bunch when the sun is straight overhead, so we have plenty of time to find a good place to ambush them as they go by."

Off to the east they could see the leading edge of the buffalo, followed by a slow moving ocean of brown. There was no end in sight. Runs with the Wind's plan to get ahead of the main herd by staying to the west had worked perfectly. Soon they would be working their way into position.

"How many do you think there are brother?"

"They are like the pebbles in a creek, you can't see the whole herd at once, so you can't count them. Those that we take for food will be replaced many times over next spring when they come back from their winter home. That is how it has been, that is how it will always be."

"I hope you're right, they sure are something to see."

"Enough talk, let's go find a place to hide. If we go now we can sneak past that bunch and go south to get ahead of them."

Slowly they led their horses along the south side of the canyon, staying in the trees and as far away from the buffalo as they could. Twice they had to stop and stand completely still while the old cow sniffed the air and tried in vain to catch sight of them. After long minutes that seemed like hours she would drop her head and go back to feeding. Once out of the canyon they were able to ride their horses and cover the ground at a much faster pace.

Jeremy was amazed by the way Runs with the Wind was able to lead him around the herd without causing them to spook. As long as there was no wind and they stayed a half mile or more away, the buffalo paid no attention to them at all. They grazed along at a slow even pace headed ever southward stopping only once to lift their huge shaggy heads long enough to identify the honking sound of a large flock of geese as they passed over the herd on their way to a warmer climate.

Still in the first hour of daylight, the boys spotted what

they had been looking for. It was a narrow spot at the south end of a large valley. Here a small stream had cut a path along a wall of shear rock. On the east side of the creek the ground was flat for a hundred paces and then rose abruptly to a height of sixty feet above the valley floor. The west bank of the creek was a sheer cliff some twenty feet high that ran north for a short distance and then turned sharply to the west following the creek. This would allow them easy access and keep the stampeding buffalo from running over them as they made their escape. The valley would funnel hundreds of the animals within easy shooting distance while the cliff would force the rest to go well to the west. Now all they had to do was work their way up the creek to the back side of the bluff without spooking the buffalo that were already nearing the ambush site.

It was three quarters of a mile to where they wanted to be, but if everything went according to plan, they had plenty of time to sneak through the trees along the stream, and still might have to wait for hours once they got there before the hunting party attacked.

Their progress was slow at best as they worked through the brush and scattered trees. They couldn't see the buffalo from where they were, but then the buffalo couldn't see them either, which made the going a little easier.

The sound of distant thunder reached Jeremy's ears as Runs with the Wind whirled his horse around.

"Run!"

Jeremy followed kicking frantically at his horses ribs. He knew something was wrong but still hadn't had time to grasp the danger of the situation they were in. As they started up the rise on the west side of the creek they could see the whole herd of buffalo was already running in blind panic, headed straight for the ridge they were on.

"We have to find a place to hide," Runs with the Wind yelled over his shoulder as he kicked his horse again and again.

Racing up to the top of the rise, they had only one small valley left between them and the safety of the mountains to the west. Their horses were laboring hard as they reached the crest only to find the valley to be filled with a raging flood of stampeding buffalo that was beginning to spill out over the edges.

The narrow passage along the creek where the boys had

attempted to make their ambush had only served to slow the progress of the stampede in that particular area, forming a pocket that left them completely surrounded.

They raced on, toward the south, inside the ever tightening circle of the great shaggy beasts that were running in terror. Dust filled the air making it almost impossible to breathe, and the thunderous roar of pounding hooves droned in their ears, covering any effort to communicate. Their horses were beginning to tire, showing signs of labored breathing, they scrambled to keep their feet under them on the soggy uneven ground.

Suddenly an old bull tripped when he lost his footing on the muddy soil, and somersaulted several times. With a broken neck, he lay immobile, creating a small dam in the unrelenting flow of the tide. A young cow darted sideways to avoid this new obstacle in her path, and collided head first into Renegade's rib cage, knocking the wind from his lungs, and the rider from his back. The horse scrambled to regain his feet, and as he did so, he vanished like a puff of smoke in the fleeing herd.

Instantly Jeremy was on his feet, running blindly through the ever tightening circle, which now was almost completely gone. His mind raced ahead, frantically searching for a place to hide from the crushing hooves that were churning up everything in their path. He felt a heavy blow against his back as one of the buffalo ran by knocking him out of the way. He rolled across the ground, arms and legs flopping about as though they were no longer solidly attached to his body. He had covered only a few feet before slamming into something solid and cold. A boulder, not much, but something to hide behind. As he scrambled around the huge stone he realized it was the beginning of a small outcropping of rocks that ran north and south forcing the buffalo to swerve either to the east or west to avoid being seriously injured or killed.

He felt a spark of hope as he looked around quickly and caught a glimpse of Runs with the Wind jumping from his horse at a dead run to scramble for the safety of the rocks. It was not to last, and his heart sank, as he watched his best friends left leg collapse when he hit the ground. In disbelief he watched as Runs with the Wind tumbled head first, just short of safety, then disappeared in the dust under the feet of the running buffalo.

Chapter Four

"It was a good hunt," Night Hawk said, surveying the large butchering site. "Antelope and Spotted Horse work well together."

"Yes, but it was Night Hawk who knew where to place the hunters for the best shots," Antelope replied.

"It could not be otherwise," Spotted Horse stated flatly, wanting to give no credit for the tremendous success to a man he considered to be his enemy. "The buffalo were so many, and so close together that any arrow shot from a hunter's bow had to find it's mark."

"Either way," Night Hawk broke in, "all things were favorable today, and it will be a good winter. The season of hunger will be short, if it comes at all."

At least two buffalo had been killed for each lodge in the village, and the women as well as many of the hunters had been working most of the day to skin the animals and cut up the huge chunks of meat so they could be spread out to cool. The livers were cut into chunks and eaten raw while they worked, and the choice portions, such as the tongue and the heart, were set aside for the hunters who had killed each animal. The meat would then be loaded onto travois made from the fresh hides and hauled back to the winter camp to be dried, jerked, or made into pemmican for the long winter ahead. On days like this, the work was extremely hard, but the rewards and satisfaction of being well prepared for the season of hunger made the task seem much less demanding.

The sun was beginning to settle in the western mountains when Little Wolf rode into the butchering camp from the south, leading two exhausted horses. The work came to a halt and a low murmur buzzed through the crowd as they gathered behind, to follow Little Wolf and the horses to the top of the ridge where Night Hawk stood watch. There was no doubt that these were the horses of Runs with the Wind and Jeremy, and two horses without riders after such a great stampede of buffalo could mean only one thing.

"Night Hawk," Little Wolf said with as much reverence in his voice as possible, "I found these horses beyond that long ridge to the south. They were headed this way at a slow walk with their reins dragging the ground. I think they had been running a long time."

"Could you tell where they came from?"

"Only for a short ways, then the tracks of the buffalo covered everything. I looked around, but I could find nothing."

"It will be dark soon, and there would be no chance of finding them, we will finish what we have to do here, and tomorrow I will go look for my sons."

Jeremy was an adopted son of the medicine man, and Runs with the Wind was his only birth son, so as long as there was a chance that either one was alive he would look, no matter how small the chance of finding them in these vast plains with all sign of their passage wiped out.

"I'll go with you," Antelope said sensing the pain in his heart, even though he refused to show it. I too feel a need to hunt for my nephews."

"I will go as well," said Spotted Horse. His desire for revenge wouldn't let him miss the moment when Night Hawk discovered the mangled bodies of his sons, and surely they must be, for no one could survive a stampede of such magnitude.

"It is settled then, tomorrow the three of us will go find my sons while the rest of you take the meat and hides back to the village. Now let us finish the work we have to do, I want to be well on my way when the sun comes up in the morning."

The men and women went back to their work with less enthusiasm. There was no longer the joking and laughter that accompanied the work after a successful hunt, only an uneasiness that each felt within themselves about the fate that surly must have befallen the two young boys.

It was a long night for Night Hawk, who sat alone on the ridge next to a small fire, chanting a prayer to the spirits for a vision that would tell him where to find his sons. For several hours he started, and restarted his prayers to the spirits, cursing himself for becoming lost in his own thoughts each time he lost his place and had to start over. By midnight he gave up and settled into his robe for a short period of fitful sleep.

The temporary camp was only beginning to stir in preparation for the long trip back to the winter camp, when Night Hawk headed south with Antelope and Spotted Horse. No one spoke as they rode toward the only spot that could possibly give them a clue about the boys location. Their only hope was that Little Wolf, in his youth and inexperience, had overlooked a clue that they might find. They were high on the ridge to the south, that Little Wolf had pointed out the day before, when the sun finally cleared the eastern horizon. From where they stood holding their horses, they could see vast amounts of the rolling broken landscape, all of which seemed to have been churned up by the hooves of the million or so buffalo that had run past here headed to a warmer, safer place further south. Half a dozen buffalo lay scattered within their view, where they had fallen from exhaustion or merely tripped, to be trampled in the unrelenting flow of the herd.

The trail that Little Wolf left behind when he led the boy's horses to the temporary butchering camp, was easy to find, and the three men picked it up without a word and began to follow it backward. Before long they found the place where he had lost the tracks in the maze of buffalo prints. They spread out, several dozen feet apart and began to circle in ever widening loops, scouring the ground for anything that looked like it might be part of a hoof print.

"The last tracks we found were where the horses left the buffalo herd and turned back toward the village. That was in that little valley over there," Night Hawk said pointing to a spot a half mile to the west. "So they would have to be somewhere between here and our temporary camp."

"There are too many places to look Night Hawk, I think we should split up."

"I think so too Antelope, you go to the east as far as you can without losing sight of me. Spotted Horse can go west the same distance and then we will all work north toward that high point there, where we will meet before dark."

Spotted Horse rode off to the west almost wishing he hadn't come along now. If either of the others found the boys first, he would miss his moment of revenge anyway and all of this would be for nothing. However if he were to find the boys first, and west was the most likely direction for them to run... "Yes," he thought "I must search everywhere for them."

With renewed enthusiasm Spotted Horse headed north weaving his way back and forth across the countryside looking under every bush and in each gully that might be deep enough to hide a body.

Long after the sun had reached its highest point, and his hopes for finding the bodies waned, Spotted Horse's sharp eyes caught a flicker of movement near a small outcropping of rocks to the northeast. With new vigor he raced across the open ground for a better look.

As he drew closer to the rocks, he realized what he had seen was a young buffalo calf standing over its mother who had apparently fallen during the rush. "Stupid thing will probably stand right there and die," he thought to himself, turning to continue his search. He was ready to ride away when he caught sight of another movement. A hand reaching out of the rocks toward him, followed by the bloody face and upper body of Runs with the Wind. A short plea for help was all he could manage before collapsing back to the earth.

Spotted Horse edged closer, now he could see Jeremy too, laying some twenty feet away at the edge of the boulder pile. Both boys appeared to be unconscious and near death. The two halves that made up Spotted Horse were in immediate conflict. One half of him wanted to rescue the boys and be counted as a hero among his people, while the other half wanted to ride away and let them die, so he could have his vengeance. "If only"... his thoughts were suddenly interrupted by the sight of a rider coming toward the rock outcropping from the east.

"Night Hawk," he said under his breath.

Slamming his heels into his pony's ribs, Spotted Horse

raced out to meet the medicine man.

"Did you find anything?" he asked reaching the other rider.

"No. I saw movement over by those rocks, but that must have been you."

"There is a buffalo calf over there, grieving over his dead mother, maybe that is what you saw."

"Well, where do you think we should look next?" Night Hawk was beginning to run short on hope.

"That valley to the northeast has a lot of places that might hide someone from a stampede such as that, let's look over there."

Spotted Horse kicked his pony and started off without even a backward glance toward the rocks where he knew the boys lay dying, he wanted to lead the medicine man as far away as he could. Night Hawk followed along, oblivious to the world around him as he began to search with his heart and spirit more than with his eyes. He didn't realize that Spotted Horse was traveling to fast to look in all the possible places that might hide the bodies of his sons or he might have been suspicious.

Chapter Five

Jeremy's ears buzzed as if they were full of hornets, while he struggled to focus his vision through the swelling and crusted blood that covered his face. His eyes met those of Spotted Horse and a feeling of relief eased the pain in his tattered body, only to be shattered a few seconds later as Spotted Horse turned and rode away at a gallop. Jeremy struggled to raise himself into a sitting position where he could lean back against one of the rocks that had undoubtedly saved his life.

He watched as Spotted Horse rode across the plains to meet another rider, who was probably out looking for them also. Jeremy had just convinced himself that Spotted Horse had gone for help, when the two of them turned and rode away toward the northeast. An empty feeling began to set in as he realized he could expect no rescue today. He had known all along that Spotted Horse didn't like Runs with the Wind, but he never thought he would leave them to die like this.

He started checking himself over for serious damage, and was pleased to find that no bones were broken and nearly all the cuts had stopped bleeding. Every part of his body was sore from the kicking and stomping hooves of the buffalo. It seemed as though no part of him had escaped the stampede unhurt.

Black and blue bruises, mixed with dried blood covered every visible part of his flesh. The part that was still covered by his tattered clothing felt about the same, and he really didn't want to look.

To weak and unsteady to get to his feet, he began to crawl in the direction he had last seen Runs with the Wind. Slowly he worked his way along, needing to know, but yet afraid to see what had made Spotted Horse lead Night Hawk away.

It was a low groan that first caught Jeremy's attention, causing him to change his direction slightly away from the rocks toward the more open country. The going was slow, painful, and difficult because of his limited ability to see, as the cuts around his eyes began to bleed again, blurring his vision. Several seconds passed as he crawled toward the moaning sound before the familiar voice stopped him.

"Where are you going brother?"

"Runs with the Wind, is that you, in the rocks?"

"Yes, but I'm in pretty bad shape."

"Then who's moaning out here?"

"It's a buffalo calf, crying over his mother, can't you see?"

"I think I got kicked in the head a couple times, my face is all swollen and my eyes won't hardly open. I can see a little, but not very well."

"Did you see Spotted Horse?"

"I thought that was him. He must really hate you, to leave us out here like this. No tellin' how long until someone else comes around here looking for us."

"Don't count on any help. Spotted Horse rode out to meet my father before he got here, and led him straight away."

"Then we'll have to walk. You said your camp was only about two days walk to the north of the buffalo, so it can't be much further from here."

"You're right, but you'll have to go alone, I can't walk."

For the first time, Jeremy noticed the large lump and odd angle to his friends left leg halfway between the knee and ankle. There was no doubt that it was broken, and needed to be set right away or Runs with the Wind would be known as Limps with the Breeze.

"We have to fix your leg, or it will never be right again."

"My leg can wait, you have more important things to do."

"Like what?"

"Like skinning that buffalo over there so we can have the robe to keep us warm tonight."

"Yea, I guess you're right, we can fix that leg in the dark if we have to, there's no telling how long it will take me to skin that buffalo by myself."

Whether from moving around a little or just from knowing that his friend was alive and with him, Jeremy wasn't sure which, but something was making him feel better and he was beginning to get his strength back. This time as he struggled to his feet, he was able to walk. Each step painful at first, getting easier as he went along.

Reaching the fallen buffalo, Jeremy noticed a small spring just behind her. Not much, but it would mean fresh water for them as long as they were here. As he knelt down to wash the crusted blood from his face, he realized that through fate the spring had also provided food and a buffalo robe to keep them warm, for it was in the little seep that the cow had lost her footing and then her life.

Squatting down to the water, he began to wash the blood and dirt away from his eyes, clearing his vision and giving back his strength. It was invigorating to feel the icy water on his skin, but daylight was beginning to fade and there was much work to be done before the dark moonless night ahead.

Unsheathing his knife he stepped over to the cow that had died the day before and began the long process of peeling the hide. Something bumped against his back and he turned to see a young calf standing over him as if to oversee the operation.

Jeremy hated to skin the cow with the calf standing there watching, but survival demanded that it be done. It might even mean that he would have to kill the calf in a few days if he was not able to salvage enough of the meat from the cow.

It was hard work as he pulled on the hide and slid the knife between the skin and muscles to sever the connecting tissue that held it in place. By the time he had one side of the buffalo skinned he had discovered two problems. First, the hide was going to weigh nearly as much he did, not to mention being extremely bulky to handle, and secondly, he couldn't do the other side without rolling her on top of the section of hide he had already taken loose.

They would have to settle for two smaller robes. He split

the hide down the center of the back and pulled it out of the way so he could roll the cow to her other side. Had she not fallen where the ground ran at a slight incline, Jeremy would not have been able to turn her over by himself. Even with the slope working in his favor, the task was almost more than he could handle.

The strain on already sore muscles made the job harder than he had imagined, and it was nearly dark by the time he had the second piece of hide removed. He grabbed both sections and had started back towards Runs with the Wind when he suddenly realized how hungry he was. Not yet hungry enough to try the raw liver again, but a couple large chunks of buffalo hump would come in handy if they could get a fire going. Meanwhile he was sure that his brother would appreciate a nice chunk of raw liver to sink his teeth into.

As he cut through the chest cavity to retrieve the liver, an idea struck him. He removed four of the longest rib bones and tossed them onto the buffalo hide. These would make an excellent splint to set Runs with the Winds broken leg.

After washing in the spring again, he wrapped the liver and two large chunks of meat in one of the pieces of hide and half carried, half dragged it back to their temporary camp. He went back for the other piece of the robe containing the rib bones and found the little buffalo calf sniffing at the hide. He would look at the tattered body of his mother and then back to the soft hide lying on the ground. The calf was confused and probably scared, but there was nothing Jeremy could do about it now.

He picked up the robe and headed back. The little buffalo took one last look at what had once been his mother and turned away to follow his instincts and that great shaggy piece of hide that had always meant comfort and security to him.

The young calf stood off to the side and watched as the two boys worked to set the broken leg back into place. They broke the four rib bones off at the proper length and tied small pieces of leather over the jagged ends. They then cut three strips of leather long enough to tie the bones securely in place once the leg was set. "Now for the hard part," Jeremy said standing over Runs with the Wind. "Once I get this pulled back into place, you'll need to be real still until the splint is tied. If you don't, the bone will slip apart, and we'll have to start over. I'm sure you won't want to do this more than one time."

Runs with the Wind lay flat on his back stretched out and as comfortable as possible, as Jeremy sat on the ground straddling his broken leg. Placing one foot gently in the crotch and the other foot in tight against the outside of the hip, Jeremy used his leverage to hold Runs with the Wind in place while he pulled on the injured leg.

It had been many hours since the leg was first broken, and the muscles had tightened around the broken ends in an attempt to keep them from moving any more. Now those same muscles were working against them as Jeremy pulled with ever increasing tension.

The pain was clearly etched in every line of Runs with the Wind's face. Each movement of muscle tissue, each time the ends of the broken bone grated against each other, each change in pressure no matter how slight, all seemed to turn his stomach. He was becoming dizzy and lightheaded when the two pieces of bone finally cleared each other to snap back into place.

Immediately the pain began to go away. Runs with the Wind laid completely still, afraid to move for fear of starting up the pain again, or having the bones slip out of place before the splint was tied securely. Jeremy placed the broken rib bones on all four sides of the leg and tied them in place with thin strips of leather. Unsure how tight it should be, or if it might swell later, he knew he would have to loosen it once in a while to allow the blood to flow.

With that finished, Jeremy spread one piece of the robe on the ground with the hair side up. He helped Runs with the Wind over onto it and spread the other half of the robe over him hair side down, making a soft cozy bed between the two pieces. He then crawled in next to his brother, and with the two of them laying close together there was plenty of robe to cover them both.

The calf watched the strange contortions his mother was making since she took on these new shapes, but at least now she was moving around some, and he was comforted by that thought as he moved closer and closer to the sleeping boys.

Chapter Six

It was almost dark by the time the three warriors gave up the search for the missing boys and turned their weary horses toward home. With all three of them looking, they had left no hiding place unchecked. Even with the ground so completely torn up with buffalo tracks, Night Hawk could see no way of overlooking them in the search. If they were still out here one of the three searchers would have found something, so they must have simply vanished, or found a safe way out of the stampede and were headed home on foot. Either way, Night Hawk was confident that his son, and his adopted son were somehow ok.

Antelope conceded that he too felt it was time to give up the search and head home. Only Spotted Horse insisted that they continue to search.

"Why does he demand that we keep looking? I thought he didn't like your sons."

"It has me concerned also," Night Hawk admitted, "but I can refuse no help right now."

"Then what should we do?"

"I want to get back to my lodge, so that I might meditate and speak to the spirits on this matter. They will know what has become of my two sons."

After a few minutes of persuading, Spotted Horse

decided to let himself be convinced that there was no hope of finding the boys, and they should turn and head home.

On the return trip there was no way for Spotted Horse to hide the look of satisfaction that he so deeply felt, so he rode alone, off to the west, pretending to continue the search as they traveled north.

It was well after daylight the next morning when they arrived at the village. Weary from the long trip, Spotted Horse and Antelope headed straight to their tepees to get some much needed rest. Standing Bear watched in silence as Night Hawk rode past without even seeing him. The sadness he felt, was as much for his friend's loss as it was for the boys who had met with such a violent end.

The people of the village were working feverishly to take care of all the meat that had been brought back the day before. Several new drying racks had been set up to help carry the loads of extra meat, and the children were busy with switches, keeping the flies as well as the camp dogs away from it as it dried. Hides were stretched out everywhere, being scraped and prepared for the tanning process. The entire village was busy when they came into view, but the work came to an abrupt halt as each friend, each neighbor, every member of this close knit village watched the unsuccessful search party ride past.

Heavy smoke from many fires hung low over the winter camp, filling the air with the tantalizing smell of roasting, and drying meat, but Night Hawk didn't notice that either as he rode straight to his lodge where his wife, Quail, already had his medicine bag ready. The many years of her marriage to Night Hawk had taught her that when things could not be solved by mere men, it was time to seek the help of the spirits, and Night Hawk was especially good at it.

Without a word of explanation he went right to it. There was no need for conversation between them, because the story was apparent when they rode in. They were back, therefore they had looked everywhere they thought the boys might have been. They brought back no bodies so the boys were not found, and quite possibly not dead. One thing was for certain, Quail would not give up hope for her two boys until she had personally prepared their bodies for the journey to the other side.

Night Hawk gathered his necessary things, and with Quails help, headed for the small medicine lodge. Quail started a small fire in the pit while Night Hawk spread out a deer skin in front of him. It was hand painted and dyed with brightly colored berry juices, in designs that only he knew the meaning of. Here he would arrange the feathers, stones, and pieces of bone which had been skillfully carved into intricate shapes. Night Hawk was not a man given to superstition who would believe that these objects had magical powers, they were merely a means of communicating with the spirits on the other side. It was like a special language, his father had taught him long ago, not so that he could speak to the spirits, who already know everything, but so they could speak to him.

His father had taught him how to temporarily leave his body and speak directly to the spirits, but that didn't always work. Sometimes they made you work for the answers through hours of interpreting the signs left with the feathers, stones, and bones. Whichever way the spirits wanted to talk to him, Night Hawk was willing to listen, and leave nothing to chance.

Slowly, as the first puff of smoke rose from the medicine lodge, Quail began the slow, methodic cadence on her drum. For the many long hours ahead, she would keep time to her husbands chanting, pausing only briefly to add a little fuel to the fire. It was a grueling task for her to sit so long maintaining the perfect rhythm, but she continued even though the sweat was running into her eyes and her arms began to cramp with fatigue.

The villagers went back to work as the drum cadence picked up speed. There was nothing they could do until the spirits had spoken to their medicine man. All any of them could do now was wait and hope for the best, with the exception of Spotted Horse. This was the moment he had been waiting for, and with Night Hawk in a venerable position, it was time to throw his plan into full action.

The first thing he needed to do, was to find his friend, Elk Talker and enlist his help. He had earned his name with his ability to talk to the big bull elk during the fall mating season, when he could convince them to walk up to within a few paces of a waiting hunter.

"Elk Talker, I've been looking for you," Spotted Horse said with a hushed urgency to his voice, "Come, we need to talk."

"Yes we do, I'm a little confused. Why were you out there hunting for Runs with the Wind, when you despise him so much?"

"That is why I went, to make sure he didn't come back."

"You didn't kill him, did you?"

"Of course not, you know that would be unforgivable among our people, but I didn't help him either, or the white boy that Night Hawk has taken in as one of his own."

"You found them?" Elk Talker asked, astonished at what his friend was confessing to.

"Keep your voice down!"

"Well did you?"

"Yes, I found them. They were stomped by the buffalo pretty bad, and without help they don't have a chance."

A sadistic smile was returning to his lips as he spoke. Already, he was beginning to savor the revenge he had waited for so long.

"You left them to die, that's the same as killing them yourself."

"No, I left them to commune with the spirits. So you see, it's not up to me, but up to the spirits whether they live or not."

"Maybe so, but remember their spirits are strong medicine. It seems nothing can harm them when they are together."

"Their spirits didn't slow down those buffalo, or lessen the blows of their hooves. I think their spirits are resting somewhere else by now."

"So why have you told me?"

"You know I intend to be the new chief as soon as I get enough followers to stand behind me. I'll need a medicine man I can trust, and that would be you."

"Why me?"

"I know you have always wanted to study under your uncle, Sun Walker, in hopes of becoming a medicine man with your mothers people, but he only has time for his two sons. Now is a good time for you to apprentice yourself with Night Hawk so that when I become Chief you can take over for him as well."

"It's a little soon, with his son disappearing only a day ago, and besides, how would I get started without angering Night Hawk?"

"Started at what?" Antelope asked, stepping around the tepee at a brisk walk. He made it seem as though he was hurrying by and had heard nothing but the very end of the conversation that was taking place.

Grasping the opportunity to recruit the aid of Night Hawks own brother-in-law seemed perfect to Spotted Horse, so he explained, "Elk Talker was planning to ask Night Hawk if he could study under him to be a medicine man. Only now with the disappearance of Runs with the Wind, he finds it an awkward time to speak of such things."

"May I speak to him for you, Elk Talker?"

"Would you?"

"I'll speak to him as soon as he is done communicating with the spirits."

"Thank you Antelope, I could not do this without your help."

"Hopefully you won't be able to do this because of my help," Antelope thought to himself as he walked away.

If only he had arrived a few moments earlier, he would have known about Spotted Horses treachery, and the way he had left the boys to die. Had he heard it all, he would have killed Spotted Horse himself, even if it did mean banishment from the tribe. As it was, all he had heard was the plan to gain control of the village from Standing Bear and Night Hawk, and for now that was enough. He would speak to Standing Bear first, and then together they could seek the advice of the medicine man.

Antelope didn't care much for Spotted Horse or his aggressive ways before, and now that he was planning to take control of the village away from the trusted men who had earned it, he liked him even less. As for Elk Talker, he wasn't sure what to think. He was a little head strong and wild at times, but generally he had been a good boy, and had grown into a respected warrior. How he had let himself be drawn into Spotted Horses evil plan was a mystery that Antelope tried to puzzle out on his way to Standing Bear's lodge.

There were many things to consider before he approached the chief with this news. He must be sure he had the facts straight in his head, and not let his personal feelings interfere with his judgement. This matter was too important for hasty decisions, and Antelope was not one to make them.

Chapter Seven

Runs with the Wind woke up shortly after daylight, struggling violently to suck in enough air to sustain life. He felt as though there was a huge weight on his chest and down the entire length of his body on the right side. Struggle as he might, the weight of the buffalo robe had him pinned to the ground as solidly as if it were a huge boulder. He tried to push the robe away from his body to no avail. His right arm was completely numb and useless, while he lacked the strength to move it with his left.

He tried to kick it away, but his right leg would not work any better than his right arm, so he kicked with his left leg, remembering as it struck solidly that it was broken. The surge of pain only served to make him struggle harder, and he grabbed a handful of hair at the top of the robe and jerked as hard as he could. It gave a little and then settled back into place. Again he jerked, screaming in agony as something smacked against his broken leg.

Suddenly the buffalo robe surged away from his body, ripping loose from the grip of his left hand and raised itself up off of the ground to turn and stare him right in the face.

"Blaaa," was all it said, looking into the astonished face of Runs with the Wind.

"I think he said, good morning mother," Jeremy said

laughing past the pain in his swollen face and split lips. "How does it feel to be a buffalo cow this morning?"

"He nearly killed me."

"The only danger you're in, is the danger of being loved too much, but me on the other hand, I'm about to starve."

"Well, start a fire, we've got more meat than we could eat in a month."

"I gathered some wood over by that creek this morning, but I don't have a flint or anything to get a fire started with."

"Yes, you do have a lot to learn brother. Hand me that stick with the small bend in it and I'll show you how to make a bow to start fires."

Runs with the Wind took his knife out of it's sheath and cut a small grove around both ends of the stick Jeremy had given him. Taking the lacing out of the moccasin he couldn't pull up over the splint on his leg, he tied both ends in the grooves he had made. Then taking a larger piece of wood that Jeremy handed to him, he used the point of his knife to make a cone shaped starter hole. Reaching into a small pouch at his waist, that Jeremy had never noticed, he produced a wooden spindle about six inches long and a small round piece of wood with a hole started on one side.

"It's time you learned to use these tools."

"Just show me how."

"First we need some dry grass and shredded bark. Break it apart until it is like pieces of hair, then roll it together in a ball, but not to tight."

Then he showed Jeremy how to wrap the leather thong around the spindle so that each time the bow was drawn back and forth the spindle would turn quickly in first one direction and then, in the other. This way the stick was always spinning, always building heat.

Back and forth, Jeremy worked the bow with one hand, while the other hand contained the little round piece of wood that held the spindle in place. Exhaustion was beginning to set in by the time the first tiny wisp of white smoke appeared. With renewed confidence he worked the bow harder, and the smoke started coming steadily.

"There's a small coal in there now Jeremy, you need to get it onto the bark and grass, and don't let it go out."

Sure enough, as Jeremy took the spindle away from the

cone shaped hole in the large piece of wood, he could see a tiny red coal in the bottom. He tried turning the wood upside down on the bark, but the ember was stuck solidly in place. With the point of his knife he pried it loose and guided it to the bed of waiting tender and watched. Nothing happened.

"You have to blow on it," Runs with the Wind said, thinking everyone should know such a simple thing.

Jeremy blew like there was no tomorrow, and watched in dismay as the little ember sailed away to land harmlessly on the ground where it blinked once and gave up its life.

"Next time try blowing softly."

Runs with the Wind could barely control his laughter, and Jeremy wasn't sure if he should be mad about the wasted effort or happy that his friend was feeling so much better. It was hard to get mad at Runs with the Wind just because he always enjoyed the little tricks that life had a habit of playing on people. "Still it would be nice if these little tricks didn't always happen to me," Jeremy thought as he prepared to start again.

"Wait a minute," Jeremy said jumping up to check his coat pockets. "Extra bullets for my gun," he said holding two in his hand as he headed back to work on the fire.

"Your gun is gone with your horse, what good will those do us now?"

"Ah, little brother, now it is time for you to learn something. The gun powder in these will make the fire start much easier."

Holding one bullet firmly in his hand, he pressed the soft lead tip sideways against a rock until it came loose, gently he poured the powder into the dry tender he had prepared earlier. He then repeated the process with the second cartridge. He had never tried this before, but was quite certain he had enough powder in the tender to get a small fire going. He picked up the bow and spindle and began to work up another ember.

"This time I will take care of the coal, and maybe we can eat today." Again Runs with the Wind's laughter was like a burr in his shirt, not really hurting him but becoming very irritating at times.

Once more the smoke started to wind up around the spindle, and Runs with the Wind rolled over to get closer to the bark where the fire would start.

"I'm ready," he said, and Jeremy eased the piece of wood

containing the tiny coal into position. Runs with the Wind used his knife to scrape the little ember into the tinder bed and leaned forward to puff gently on it.

Even Jeremy was surprised when the powder caught and flashed up in Runs with the Wind's face singeing his hair and eyebrows.

"You're right," Jeremy said, "you do handle that much better than me."

This time it was Jeremy who tried to control his laughter as the two boys put together the fire that would cook their first meal since the stampede.

Chapter Eight

Antelope wondered aimlessly through the village talking to everyone as he passed. Not about anything in particular, just making conversation so as not to arouse any suspicion in the minds of Spotted Horse and Elk Talker, who were still watching him, trying to decide if he had heard more than he let on.

"He knows nothing," Spotted Horse sneered, "he is an old man past his time. He thinks the old ways are the only way, besides, he's not clever enough to figure out our plans even if we sat down and explained them to him."

"Do not under estimate him Spotted Horse, Antelope may be getting long in winters, but he is a worthy adversary under any terms."

As the two men continued their conversation, Elk Talker began to wonder if it was a good plan after all. He knew the part about apprenticing himself to Night Hawk was good, because it was what he really wanted, and Runs with the Wind had never shown any real interest in following in his father's footsteps. But to try to seize control of the village, before the older and more experienced men were ready to relinquish their authority might not be a wise decision, it might even be a very dangerous one. Now that Spotted Horse had left Runs with the Wind and his blood brother Jeremy to die out on the plains, it made Elk Talker wonder exactly what kind of chief he would be. Certainly someone with that responsibility should put the welfare of his people first, all of his people, regardless of personal conflicts.

"I must find time to think this out," he said to himself as Spotted Horse walked away.

As soon as the cadence of the drums stopped, Antelope and Standing Bear headed for Night Hawks medicine lodge. They stopped briefly at the entrance to announce their presence, and Quail led them in.

The three men sat cross legged, facing each other with the fire in the middle. The air was still heavy with the scents of sage and green cedar boughs that had been added to the flames.

"We must deal with this matter very carefully," Standing Bear told his two closest friends. "Until we know who is with them, we must keep this between the three of us."

"It's Elk Talker that bothers me most," Night Hawk replied, "I had hopped he would come to this decision under better circumstances."

"Will you turn him down?"

"No, but I'll make him earn every bit of information he gets."

"What about your son?"

"Runs with the Wind hasn't got the patience for it, or the interest."

"Speaking of your sons," Standing Bear broke in, "have the spirits told you how to find them yet?"

"No, they told me only that my sons would come back with the buffalo, for this I am happy."

"How will they survive the winter?" Standing Bear asked, genuinely concerned. "They have no horses, no food, and no weapons with which to hunt or defend themselves."

"All I know, is what the spirits told me. They said my sons would return with the buffalo, and I am not one to question the spirits. Separately, both of my sons have become men in their own right, but together, their spirit medicine is stronger than any I have ever seen. When the buffalo return you will understand that what I say is true."

"I have no doubt that what you say is true Night Hawk, but it would be almost impossible for anyone to survive a winter under those conditions."

"It is up to the spirits now, they have shown me that

there is nothing we can do but wait."

"Well Night Hawk, how do you think we should deal with this other matter then?"

"I believe we should remove some of the leaders strength by showing his followers what a hard trail he has chosen to follow. Antelope, bring Elk Talker to me, I think we should start with him."

Standing Bear could see by the smile on Night Hawks face, that Elk Talker was in for a rough time. He would be given plenty of opportunity to succeed, and taught all of the skills necessary to be a medicine man, but the position was not going to be handed to him. It would take years to learn all the skills and information necessary for the job.

Elk Talker was excited to have been summoned so soon after his request, especially after the recent disappearance of Runs with the Wind. No matter though, it was not his concern. If the spirits wanted Runs with the Wind to live, he would, if not, life would go on without him.

"Elk Talker," Night Hawk said with all the dignity befitting the occasion of accepting an apprentice, "it has been brought to my attention that you wish to take on the duties of a medicine man's apprentice."

Yes uncle," he replied showing as much dignity and respect for the man as for the position he held.

"Then we shall begin. First you must purge yourself and seek acknowledgment from the spirits. For this task, you must go to the edge of the village where you will stand looking into the heavens through the night and into the day that follows. You will do this while chanting, "tell me spirits am I worthy," until they answer you one way or the other.

"And when they answer me, what should I tell them?"

"Tell them nothing. You are to listen, and learn from the experience. A medicine man does not tell the spirits anything, he seeks help and guidance from their great knowledge."

"Yes uncle," Elk Talker replied and he turned to walk out into the chill of the autumn night. The clouds were heavy and the promise of snow was in the air, but this could not dampen the spirits of Elk Talker. He was finally on his way to begin the undertaking of his dreams. It could snow, rain, or hail for all he cared, as long as the spirits acknowledged his presence, the price would not be to great.

"He's really a good boy," Night Hawk said, "he just needs to learn a little more about what is really important in life."

The three men watched as Elk Talker walked to the outer edge of the village, wearing nothing but a loin cloth and his moccasins.   He stood with his head back and his arms out stretched chanting the prayer Night Hawk had told him. Within minutes he had slipped into a melodic cadence and was completely   oblivious to the tiny snowflakes that were falling all around him.

"He is a good boy," Standing Bear agreed, "it's to bad he had to get mixed up with the young trouble makers."

"Yes, under other circumstances I think he would have made a fine medicine man some day."

"Tell me Night Hawk, do you think you can help me come up with such a grueling task for one who wants to be chief?"

"I'm sure we can come up with something that would be suitable."

"Good, these young ones who have turned their backs on the old ways need to be taught a lesson."

The temperature was beginning to drop and the three older men returned to the warmth and comfort of the medicine lodge.   Here they could speak freely without fear of being interrupted or overheard.   They sipped a hot herbal tea, tempered with just enough mint to give it an interesting flavor, while they told each other funny stories from the past, that had already been told time and time again. Yet it was the art of telling the stories that made them always interesting, adding small variations, or telling a story from opposite points of view could make all the difference in the world. Even so, this was only a small part of their entertainment as they took turns going out into the falling snow to check on the young apprentice, who's determination and will seemed as strong after several hours, as it had in the beginning.

Chapter Nine

The small fire caught quickly, and grew steadily as the boys added fuel from the stack of wood Jeremy had carried up from the creek bed. Two of the longer sticks had been sharpened to a fine point and were soon holding the chunks of meat Jeremy had salvaged from the buffalo carcass the night before.

"I think we'll move camp today," Jeremy said as he turned the meat. "We'll need more firewood to keep warm at night, and we're going to need to dry a bunch of this meat before it spoils."

"I won't be much help, with this leg broken, and the rest of my body feeling like it is."

"That's ok, I didn't figure on moving to far anyway. There's a nice spot over next to the creek where we can have everything we need while were curing enough meat to last us until you are well enough to travel."

"That might be a long time."

"We'll worry about that later, right now all I'm interested in is that chunk of buffalo meat on the end of this stick."

The juices were beginning to drip from the meat into the fire, sizzling and sending up little tendrils of smoke that made Jeremy's mouth water in anticipation. The meat was far from cooked, but the thought of eating it raw became more feasible with every whiff of the tantalizing aroma.

When the meat was little more than half done, Jeremy could wait no longer. Remembering the succulent taste of the buffalo hump that Runs with the Wind had prepared for him the previous summer, he couldn't wait any longer. Slicing off a generous portion, he sank his teeth into it like a starving animal, ignoring the grease that ran down his chin, to drip into the grass at his feet. Never before had food tasted any better. Only after their stomachs were full to the point of bursting, did they return their thoughts to moving the camp.

It would only be a short walk to the creek for Runs with the Wind if his leg was well, but with the condition he was in, it seemed to be an almost insurmountable task. When the bone in his leg broke, it didn't come out through the skin, but it did move around a lot tearing muscle tissue all around the break. The slightest amount of pressure applied to the left foot would cause lights to explode in his head and his stomach to tie into knots.

The two boys stood together, side by side as Runs with the Wind struggled against the pain to clear his head. With his arm around Jeremy's shoulder and Jeremy's arm around his waist they were able to cover short distances of ground before the pain became so intense that Runs with the Wind would have to stop. No matter what they tried his leg seemed to bang against Jeremy or the ground sending shock waves of pain through his body.

"Wait a minute," Jeremy said, "I have an idea."

"For what."

"For helping you walk."

"I would need another leg for that."

"That's my idea, you can use one of mine."

"Big brother, I think you got kicked in the head much harder than we first thought."

"No you don't understand, it's a game we played on picnics back home. We had races where two runners were on each team, only they stood side by side and tied the right leg of one runner to the left leg of the other runner to make one runner with three legs."

"Maybe you should find a place to rest, I don't think you're well."

"This will work, all I need is something to bind our legs together."

He helped Runs with the Wind to a comfortable position on the ground and turned back toward their pitiful little campsite. Basically they had nothing because all of their belongings were tied on the horses when they ran off. He would have to cut down one of the pieces of buffalo robe.

His sharp hunting knife sliced easily through the skin as he cut away a section of one. It was a foot wide and long enough to wrap around their legs almost two times. He then began slicing strips that were about one inch wide so he would have a way of tying their legs together.

He took the pieces back to where he had left Runs with the Wind resting in the grass. He helped the smaller boy back to his feet and began to bind their legs together. Jeremy was taller and Runs with the Wind had to raise his leg a little to get their knees at the same height. He wrapped the wide strip of leather around their legs as tight as possible, and used two of the thin strips to tie it securely in place. He then handed another thin strip to Runs with the Wind.

"Ok, little brother, tie your ankle to my leg so it won't bang around as we walk."

"How tight?"

"As tight as you can stand it. It shouldn't take us long to get to the creek."

Once the knots were finally secure, the boys began testing their weight on them. Everything seemed to hold and they took their first step together. Gingerly testing their balance, they took a small step forward on the legs that were bound together. Not a long step, but forward progress, none the less. Next came the hard part, stepping forward on their free legs with only Jeremy's right leg to balance both of them. It was wobbly at first and very uncomfortable, but caused almost no pain to the injured leg. Each step forward became easier than the last, until they developed a routine that allowed them to make steady even movements as they hobbled across the open ground.

The buffalo calf watched through confused eyes as he tried to make some sense out of the strange activities, but his mother had never led him wrong in the past so all he could do was continue to follow her scent and this new creature she had become.

When they reached the little clearing that Jeremy had picked out for a temporary campsite along the creek, the boys undid the binding that held them together and Runs with the Wind sank to the ground in exhaustion.

"It worked," he said looking back across the path they had traveled. Some two hundred paces had taken them almost an hour and all of his reserved energy, but they were in a much better situation now.

"Yea, but we'll never get home that way little brother. I guess we can stay here for awhile."

"You can go for help."

"Go where? I don't know my way around out here, it all looks the same to me, I'd be lost before I got started. Besides even if I did find help, I would never find my way back here. No, I think we'd best stick together."

"Ok, but we're going to have to finish butchering that buffalo and build drying racks to cure the meat."

"Fine, I'll bring the rest of our things over here and do the butchering, you can build the racks and do the drying."

"You need to start another fire," Runs with the Wind said grinning.

Jeremy was not looking forward to going through the ordeal of building a fire again. If he had a tin cup or something like that he could simply carry some coals to the new location and have a fire in a few minutes. All he needed was...

"I'll be back in a minute," he said picking up the wide leather strip that had held their legs together. He went back to the old campsite and bent down to the fire. Using two small sticks he reached into the bed of coals that remained and placing one stick on each side of a large coal, he lifted it out of the fire and placed it on the leather. He folded the ends up to form a sling to cradle the coal, and headed back to the new camp.

"Here is your fire," he said as he dropped the coal on the ground. "All you have to do is bring it back to life."

"I'll get the fire going and start building the drying racks, you just bring me some meat to put on them."

"I'll go get our sleeping robes and use them to carry the meat to you. I'll be back with the first load in a little while."

When Jeremy got back to the old camp, the buffalo calf was already there, nuzzling the two sections of robe made from his mothers hide. He didn't like it when she laid on the ground so flat and unmoving and was trying to get her up to play.

As Jeremy grabbed the two sections and threw them, one

over each shoulder, the calf perked up and followed quickly behind as he headed for what was left of the carcass.

The calf became confused again as Jeremy spread the two sections of hide out so that the hair side was to the ground. He nuzzled them again and could find no sign of life. He stepped closer and sniffed of Jeremy, who by now was covered with the scent of the cow buffalo. That was better, now the calf could find the scent of his mother, mixed with the scent of life itself, something she had been lacking the last two days. The buffalo calf felt a contentment he had not known since the stampede began a couple days earlier. Now as Jeremy began slicing off huge chunks of meat, the calf was content to graze on the nearby prairie grass.

The rest of the day passed pretty much without incident until it was nearly dark. Jeremy had just picked up the last load of meat for drying and was headed for the fire. They had a pile of meat that would take at least two days to dry if they worked at it hard, but it would supply them with enough meat for a month or more. They both knew they would need to find some plants to eat also, because meat alone wouldn't keep them healthy. It would however keep them alive for a long time.

As he settled down by the drying fire with his pack full of meat, a wolf howled off to the west. Another wolf answered from the south, and a third from the northwest, not very far away.

"If they smell the meat we're in trouble," Jeremy said.

"The wind is blowing toward the southwest, it is a pretty good breeze and I'm sure those two down there will pick up the scent."

"What can we do?"

"I'm not sure, but we better find something to use for weapons.

Chapter Ten

The sun was lifting itself over the eastern horizon when Elk Talker turned to walk back toward the medicine lodge where Night Hawk was once again talking to Antelope and Standing Bear. His skin was covered with the goose flesh that accompanies the loss of body heat in such cold weather, causing his teeth to chatter together as he tried to repeat to himself one more time, the speech he had rehearsed over and over in his mind. He didn't want to go against Spotted Horse, who had been his friend since youth, but his conscious would let him do no less.

The three men could see the distress that weighed heavy on Elk Talker as he made his way along. It was apparent that he was struggling with himself over a matter of some importance.

"Good morning Elk Talker, have the spirits spoken to you yet?" Night Hawk asked.

"I'm not sure, but I have spoken to myself all night, and I have decided that I must unburden my spirit with you and Standing Bear before I can continue."

"Come inside and sit by the fire, we can talk there while you get warm."

Night Hawk led the way back into the medicine lodge, followed by Standing Bear. Elk Talker went next and Antelope pulled the door cover into place and secured it from the inside.

When all were seated around the fire, Night Hawk handed a cup of hot tea to Elk Talker who gratefully wrapped his cold fingers around the warm container. As he sipped the hot liquid he could feel the warmth of it travel down his throat to the pit of his empty stomach. The warmth penetrating through his body caused him to shiver uncontrollably, making it impossible for him to speak with all the dignity the circumstances required.

Night Hawk felt a twinge of guilt as he watched the young man sipping the hot tea. Maybe his desires of becoming a medicine man were pure, even if his loyalties were confused.

The three men waited patiently for the shivering to subside enough for Elk Talker to begin.

"I have information," he said, not knowing how his confession would be accepted among the tribal leaders. "I think Runs with the Wind and Jeremy are alive."

"I think so too," said Night Hawk, "I had a vision that they would return with the buffalo."

"But I know they didn't die in the stampede," he insisted.

"How could you know this?" Antelope asked, "You were with me during the hunt, and you came home with the main party."

"It is how I know, that burdens my spirit," Elk Talker said, unable to look the three men in the face.

"Tell us what you know for sure, and we will decide together what to do with the information you have," Standing Bear replied, as he watched the young man with renewed interest.

"I would not have considered going along with Spotted Horse's plan if I had not wanted to be a Medicine man so bad," he stammered.

"We know about Spotted Horse's plan to take over the leadership of our tribe, we just don't know how he intends to do it, or who is helping him," Standing Bear spoke so evenly that it stunned Elk Talker. He thought this would be news that would cause great distress among the leaders, and they sat around discussing it as calmly as the weather.

"I don't know much," Elk Talker began again, his voice trembling more from apprehension and embarrassment now, than the cold, "I wasn't a part of his plan until yesterday when he told me you would need an apprentice."

"You didn't know I needed one?"

"No, I thought Runs with the Wind would be your apprentice."

"He doesn't have the interest, but what made you think that I would accept you now?"

"I thought after a while with your son not returning, you would remember I was interested."

"You said you knew he was not killed in the stampede, why did you think he wouldn't come home?"

"Spotted Horse told me he wouldn't live long enough to get home."

Standing Bear jumped to his feet with a scowl of rage crossing his face. "He intends to kill the boys before they can return?"

"No, he intends to let the spirits decide their fate. He said he would not raise a hand to kill one of his own people, even one that he hates, but he would not lift a hand to help that one either."

"So exactly what are you trying to tell us?" Antelope asked.

"Spotted Horse found the boys, he saw they were hurt bad and had no food or warm clothing, and he left them to die."

"Where?"

"He wouldn't say where they were."

"They have to be close to where the mountains join the prairie, that's where Spotted Horse looked," Night Hawk said, "my vision showed me they would return with the buffalo, but I must still do everything I can to find them. At the same time, we must consider how to deal with Spotted Horse and his followers, whoever they might be."

"I have thought about that too," Elk Talker said, "It was a long night, and I had time to think about a lot of things. You can send Spotted Horse back out to look for your sons. Tell him you had a vision and they are alive. He will have to take only his closest friends with him in case they run across your sons. We can follow them to see if they look or not, and they might even lead us right to them if he's worried that they are alive."

"I have heard enough," Standing Bear snarled. "Spotted Horse no longer has a place in this village. I will ask the council of elders to banish him forever."

"Wait," Night Hawk cut in, "we must first give him an

opportunity to lead us to my sons."

"You are right Night Hawk, if we banish him now, he will have no reason not to ride out and kill the boys himself. We must make him believe that we trust him until they are safely home."

"We have a better idea where to look for them now that we know Spotted Horse actually found them. We had only split up for a few hours and were never that far apart. We must get started right away."

"I will go find Spotted Horse," said Standing Bear, "and send him to search again. I will be very interested to know who he picks to go with him."

Antelope got to his feet and followed the chief out of the door. "I will take my horse and be waiting over that ridge," he said pointing to the southwest. "When Spotted Horse and his friends leave, I will be like a shadow to them."

"Maybe you should take two or three men with you," Standing Bear said. "Any man in the village would be willing to help find the boys."

"No, I can travel faster, and quieter alone. Besides until we know for sure who is with him in this scheme, I want to talk to no one about it."

"What if he goes to the boys? What if there is trouble?"

"If there is trouble, I will kill Spotted Horse, and there will be no more trouble."

Without another word he swung to his pony's back and rode out of camp toward the north. He rode well out of sight before turning to circle south. He pushed his horse hard to be sure he was in position in plenty of time.

Standing Bear watched as he rode away, wondering what was becoming of the people, that they could consider taking the life of one of their own kind so easily. These thoughts weighed heavy on his mind as he turned to go look for Spotted Horse, who was never hard to find. Anywhere young people gathered to talk when there was no work to be done, you could be sure he would be among them.

Spotted Horse stood talking to Little Wolf, which surprised Standing Bear completely. He knew of no friendship between these two who were so different. Little Wolf was a tra-ditionalist who believed strictly in the old ways, while Spotted Horse was something of a radical. Standing Bear was beginning to worry about the loyalties of Little Wolf, when he realized that not far beyond the boys, Morning Dove was working over a buffalo hide. She and Little Wolf were both four summers younger than Spotted Horse, which made it hard for Little Wolf to hold her attention whenever he was around.

"Spotted Horse," Standing Bear called, "come here, I need to speak to you."

"What is it my Chief?"

How can he act so polite and so respectful when, treachery is his driving motive, Standing Bear thought.

"I want you to go back and look for Runs with the Wind and Jeremy."

"Shouldn't that be left to Night Hawk and Antelope?"

"Normally it would be, but they have had no sleep for several days and Night Hawk had a vision that the boys were alive and trying to get home. You know where to go to look for them, so I want you to take a few men with you and go search one more time."

"But we looked everywhere."

"Look again, if they are alive and moving around there will be signs."

Spotted Horse hadn't considered that possibility. It had been a few days since the stampede and if either one of them was able to move around much, they would be a lot easier to find. He would have to go to keep others from doing it, but he could take only his most loyal friends, Coyote Track, and Red Fox, because besides himself and Elk Talker who was undergoing the initiation rights of an apprentice medicine man, these were the only two he trusted with the information he had.

"I will be ready to go soon. I will tell Coyote Track and Red Fox to bring enough food for three days. If there is any sign of them, we will find it."

"It is good," Standing Bear said, and he turned to walk back to the medicine lodge where Night Hawk waited with his new apprentice.

Elk Talker rose to his feet as Standing Bear came into the lodge. "I will go back and begin my chant to the spirits again," he said, "now that my heart is unburdened, maybe they will speak to me."

"They have spoken to us both, Elk Talker. They showed you the way to do what was best for your people, and they showed me that you would make a good medicine man someday."

Night Hawk then turned his attention to Standing Bear, "Did you find him?"

"Yes, he is taking Coyote Track and Red Fox with him, and Antelope is already on their trail," Standing Bear said.

"Coyote Track, and Red Fox. I never would have expected them to be in on this."

"I too was surprised, but in these matters you can't always tell who your friends are. If you want to follow along behind, I would like to go with you."

"There will be no need for us to follow, Antelope is one of the best trackers in the village, as well as one of the most capable warriors, he should be able to handle any problems that he comes up against."

Chapter Eleven

Jeremy searched around until he found two long, solid, oak sticks, that would make decent clubs, but that would not be nearly enough to keep off a pack of wolves. He took them back to the fire and started gathering fist size rocks from the creek bed. Using his shirt as a container to carry the smooth round stones, he made several trips back and forth until he had a large pile gathered.

"This breeze is carrying the scent of cooking meat a long way Jeremy," Runs with the Wind said, "we need to cover the smell."

"How?"

"I think if you go downwind a little ways and start a prairie, fire the wolves might run away. It will have to be a big one."

"It's worth a try," Jeremy said as he pulled some tall prairie grass and began wrapping it tightly around a stick. "I'll make a torch and start several little fires from there, to there," he said pointing first to the east and then swinging his arm south until he was pointing almost west.

"You better get started, they're not far away."

Jeremy lit his torch in the cooking fire and headed south out of camp. He waded across the little stream that ran from west to east and followed it a short distance down stream before walking out of the rocky creek-bottom and back onto the open prairie again. He walked another thirty steps before lighting the first fire. It caught quickly and began to grow rapidly with the help of the gentle breeze. He started moving to the southwest, and started a new fire after only a few more steps. He continued the process until he had made a large half circle around their camp. By the time he got back to where Runs with the Wind sat, the fires had joined into one large line, expanding to an ever increasing length as it fed hungrily along the prairie grass. Bright yellow and orange flames jumped toward the sky, proclaiming their new life as they devoured everything in their path. The fires spread to the east and west as they made their way southward. The flames would continue to grow until they met some natural obstacle, such as a creek or a rocky ridge where it could not burn through, or the wind might simply change directions turning it back on itself where there was no fuel left to burn.

"If it doesn't rain or snow tonight, that should keep anything from coming that way," Jeremy said, "but what about the one we heard up to the north?"

"We can't take a chance on setting that kind of fire on this side of the creek, if it got into the trees, we'd be trapped. We need to keep a lot of wood handy and a fire going all night. With some luck he won't come this way."

Late into the night the boys took turns resting and taking care of the fires that were curing their food supply. The Prairie fire had burnt feverishly for several hours until a change in the wind, which shifted to blow north, had nearly stopped it in its tracks. Small fires could still be seen far to the south, but they were isolated and slowly dying out.

Both boys were resting easier now, as was their new companion. The buffalo quietly lay in the grass, sometimes sleeping and sometimes watching them work, and sometimes it was hard to tell which.

Somewhere between late night and early morning, while Jeremy was tending the fire, his eyes slipped shut. "I'll just rest my eyes for a moment," he told himself. He awoke with a start. Something was wrong and he wasn't quite sure what it was. His fires were almost out, only glowing embers remained, but what sent shivers up his spine was the bleating sounds coming from the buffalo calf. He tossed a few small sticks on the fire and they flared up instantly, lighting the silhouette of a large black wolf creeping closer and closer toward the three of them. The buffalo calf backed up against the thick brush that sheltered their camp on the east side, nearly stepping on Runs with the Wind as he sat up clutching his club in his left hand and a rock in his right.

Jeremy's club lay at his feet as he began hurling rock after rock at the intruding wolf. The reflexes of the wolf were too quick for the stones, and he leaped out of the way as each one flew past. Steadily he advanced on his prey, trying to get close enough for that one fatal leap that would bring down his rock throwing adversary. Jeremy's necessary concentration was suddenly shattered by a low growl off to his left.

"There's more than one," he said, trying to look in that direction while focusing his attention on the positive threat in front of him.

Runs with the Wind knew they were in serious danger and unable to defend themselves from the wolves on all sides, there wasn't much he could do from where he sat with the limited weapons they were using.

The second wolf made a charge out of the dark and Jeremy adjusted his throw well enough to catch it in the ribs. The stone made a hallow sounding thud causing the injured wolf to dart back into the safety of darkness.

The fire was dying down again, making it extremely difficult to keep track of the wolves with only the sound of low growling, which seemed to be coming from everywhere, to give away their location.

Darkness was the enemy and daylight was still a long time coming. Runs with the Wind had to make a decision, would it be better to try to fight off the pair of wolves or take their chances with a fire on their own side of the creek.

Again a wolf rushed in close, too close, he was only a few feet away before Jeremy's rock turned him back. The boys needed help, and they needed light, and Runs with the Wind gave them both as he shoved one of the last flaming embers into the thick dry brush behind him.

The flames caught quickly, and Runs with the Wind dragged himself across the ground to where Jeremy stood over his dwindling pile of stones. The flames leaped high under the influence of a growing breeze that pushed the fire toward them.

The added light and smoke from the fires confused the wolves and held them at bay while they waited for their prey to run out into the open to escape the flames.

The grass was sparse in their camp but the wind made it a constant battle for the boys to beat back the fire that tried to swallow them up. Smoke began to billow around them as they beat out small fires. The buffalo calf raced out into the darkness to escape the flames, to return shortly, chased by the pair of hungry wolves who lost their courage at the last minute when confronted by the heavy smoke and fire.

The fire progressed rapidly to the north and along the creek bottom to the south leaving only a narrow passage way to the west for possible escape.

Within minutes the boys were on the island of sparse grass with fire all around. An occasional spark would land in their campsite starting a small flame which the boys quickly learned to extinguish by covering them with a buffalo robe.

The clearing they defended was about twenty feet across and growing to the north as the fires burned out behind the main thrust of the flames. The passageway to the west also began to open in the same manner, and the wolves decided to take advantage of it.

Slowly they came forward, snarling and growling, they closed in staying low to the ground. The fire had not been enough, and now served only to light up the area where the final confrontation would take place.

The buffalo calf stood shaking in terror with no place to run. It's two most deadly enemies had it totally surrounded with no means of escape. The two boys prepared for the inevitable attack which was getting closer all the time.

As if on an unvoiced signal, that both wolves knew instinctively from years of hunting together, they separated to attack from two different angles. The charge came instantly and Jeremy's rock turned away the wolf that came at him. The other wolf went straight for Runs with the Wind who was already on the ground. He was on his knees despite the pain, and the animal instincts of the wolf sensed his adverse situation. He let the wolf come in close before throwing his rock. It glanced off the side of the wolf's head as it leaped toward him. Stunned by the blow, the wolf landed short of it's mark and received a terrible blow from a well placed club, that ended its life.

Jeremy made the mistake of turning to see if Runs with the Wind was all right and the second wolf leaped on him from behind sending the two of them rolling through the grass away from help. Jeremy rolled to his back and the wolf was immediately on him again. He hit the wolf in the head with his left fist. The animal showed almost no sign of the blow and grabbed the arm just above the wrist. His large white fangs sank into the flesh as he shook his head back and forth.

Jeremy was sure he had made a fatal mistake that would allow the wolf to overpower him totally. He struggled to keep those flashing fangs away from his throat, but the instincts of all animals run strong in a fight, whether predator or prey, and just as things looked hopeless, a sharp buffalo hoof caught the wolf in the ribs, sending him flying through the air. The snapping of rib bones was followed almost immediately by painful howling, as the wolf landed in the burning embers where Runs with the Wind had first started the fire.

The injured wolf scrambled through the dying flames and headed across the creek away from the fire.

Runs with the Wind crawled toward Jeremy, afraid of what he would find. Jeremy was laying on his back, unmoving, with eyes wide and glazed.

His father had told him what shock could do to a person but he had never seen it for himself. As he reached for Jeremy's arm to examine the wound, his friend sat bolt upright and opened his mouth for a scream that wouldn't come out, and fainted dead away. The past few days of pain and struggle for survival had taken quite a toll on him physically as well as psychologically, and the wolf attack was just more than his mind was willing to cope with.

Runs with the Wind bandaged the wounds on Jeremy's arm with strips of cloth cut from the tail of his shirt, and settled him into a comfortable position where he could get some much needed rest.

Runs with the Wind stood watch the rest of the night and well into the day. He had a few rocks left and his club at the ready even though he was sure they were no longer in danger with the prairie burnt for miles in all directions.

Chapter Twelve

The last thing Spotted Horse wanted to do today was to go back out on the plains for three days pretending to look for the boys he didn't want to find. Coyote Track and Red Fox were also preparing their things, with pretty much the same thoughts in mind. Neither of them had anything against Runs with the Wind or Jeremy, but with the inevitable changes that were coming to the village they could not let their personal feelings stand in the way of necessary loyalties.

Spotted Horse would be Chief someday, and he would remember who his friends were. More importantly he would remember who was not. It would be best to go along willingly and hope they didn't see the boys at all, or if they did come across them, that they would already have crossed over into the after life, leaving them free of any guilt.

News traveled fast among the villagers, and when word got around that another search party was going out, Little Wolf and some of the other young men showed up ready for the long trail ahead.

"Where are you going Little Wolf?" Spotted Horse asked.

"With you, we thought you could use the help."

"We need no help."

"It is good," Standing Bear cut in, "more eyes can look more places."

"All right," Spotted Horse said, realizing that his task of pretending to search was getting harder all the time. He would have to be sure to split the search party up before he got close to where he had last seen them.

Coyote Track and Red Fox could feel the tension in the air as they turned away from the village. The situation he had gotten himself into was getting worse all the time. With so many people looking for the two boys, sooner or later someone would find them, and if they were still alive there was a chance that they had seen him before he rode away to meet Night Hawk.

"I should have clubbed them both in the head, and let the buffalo be blamed for their deaths," Spotted Horse thought to himself, "then it would be over and I wouldn't be here now."

Spotted Horse, Coyote Track, and Red Fox, rode along in silence as the group headed south, while Little Wolf and his friends talked constantly about the possibility of finding their friends and where the best places to look would be.

Spotted Horse was getting irritated at the constant chatter among his unwanted help, and trying to decide what to do about it when he realized that the clouds he had been watching to the south were not clouds at all, but smoke. A huge prairie fire burning itself out as the constantly changing winds pushed it back on already burnt grasses.

As they rode to the top of a ridge for a better look, they could see a few small fires still burning where the brush was thickest, and miles and miles of blackened earth where the fire had already devoured everything living or dead.

"Do you think they started it?" Little Wolf asked.

"No," Spotted Horse said too quickly, trying to come up with another reason for the fire. "It was probably started by white settlers passing through, they sometimes leave their fires burning when they move on."

"Maybe," said Little Wolf, "but I think we should look around the edge of the fire just in case. If they started it to signal for help, they'll be on the edge of the burn somewhere."

"You might be right," Spotted Horse said recognizing a chance to get rid of his unwanted help. "You three go along the fire to the east, and work south along that edge looking for tracks. We'll go to the west and do the same. We will meet you on the south side of the burn."

Little wolf and his friends began the process of working

their way around the fire. He was pretty sure that the boys wouldn't be on this end but he was leaving nothing to chance. They watched for sign as they rode along but didn't waste time searching as hard as they would on the southeast side of the fire. More likely whoever started it would be down that way.

Spotted Horse, Coyote Track, and Red Fox started to the west in the same manner. Once out of sight, they stopped as Spotted Horse explained his plan.

"Continue around the way you are going, but hurry, I don't want them to beat us to the source of the fire. I'm going to cut through and meet you on the other side."

Coyote Track and Red Fox nodded dutifully to Spotted Horse and continued the mock search at a faster pace than before. Spotted Horse turned due south and rode toward the spot where he had seen Runs with the Wind and Jeremy lying in the dirt by the outcropping of rocks. He kicked his horse into a lope knowing that he must be the first to reach them. He wasn't sure how to handle the situation, but he could decide on that later when he was sure what the situation was.

For several miles he rode through the ashes of the burnt prairie grass, passing small streams and gullies where the thicker brush and small trees were still smoldering. Everything looked the same, more so now than ever. With everything burnt there was nothing but black and grey ashes as far as the eye could see.

Unsure of his exact location he rode to the top of a small rise for a better view. From here he could see the rocks where he had left the boys to die, but not the edge of the fire. Wherever it had started, it had swept through here like a summer storm burning almost everything. Only along the stream did any bushes and small trees survive the fire, and even they were severely scorched by the heat. "It would be impossible for them to survive in the path of such a fire," he thought, "if the flames didn't kill them, surly the smoke would have suffocated them.

He could see that everything had burnt, with the exception of a couple places along the creek. Here the fire had found easier passage around, but those places were small covering only a few feet in each direction.

He watched patiently for any sign of movement or life. It was still a long ways to the rocks, but if they were moving around he would see them, and if they had headed for camp he would have crossed their trail. They had to still be down there, most likely dead, but Spotted Horse wasn't willing to take that chance. If they had somehow survived, it would not be his tracks that led others to find them. Better to stay as far away as possible and head south to meet with the others.

As he turned his horse to ride back down off of the rise his eyes caught movement. Not down by the rocks but on his back trail. Someone was following him, and trying not to be seen. Had it not been for everything being burnt he probably wouldn't have noticed the tan horse that far away, and the rider would be able to follow at his leisure.

Spotted Horse rode back down the ridge the way he had come and waited for the rider to show himself. Had he not stopped on that rise for a while to look around he would not have realized that Antelope was on his trail. It was indeed fortunate that he had decided not to go down for a closer look.

"Antelope!" Spotted Horse yelled the greeting to surprise the man who didn't yet realize he had been seen. "I'm glad you decided to join the search."

The older man was furious with himself for getting caught off guard, but tried to show some relief in his voice and expression as he answered, "I didn't want to be left behind, so I came as soon as I could."

They talked for a few minutes, each man being extremely careful of what he said. Both suspected that the other man had an idea of what his opponent was up to and it became a silent battle of wits with neither man giving ground.

"I was headed south when I saw you coming along behind me," Spotted Horse finally said, "I waited so you could help me look."

"Where did the others go?" Antelope asked.

"They went around the two sides of the burn to look for sign. I wanted to ride straight through to the point where the fire started to see if they had started it to signal for help."

"Then let us go."

Antelope hated to admit it, but it did make sense, and even seemed that Spotted Horse was doing everything he could to help find the boys. Something was wrong though, and Antelope would not let down his guard until he figured out what it was.

Chapter Thirteen

It was late afternoon when Runs with the Wind opened his eyes to the bright yellow sun. He laid still for several minutes trying to focus his vision. That's when he saw Spotted Horse on the ridge off to the west. His pinto horse was unmistakable, as was the arrogant way he sat on it's back.

He was sure Spotted Horse was trying to locate them to be sure they were dead. If he wanted to help, he would have done that days before when he was here last. Runs with the Wind lay perfectly still not wanting to give away his location.

Jeremy and the buffalo calf both lay sleeping close by. It had been an exhausting night, with the wolf attack and their own fire both trying to do them in, and fatigue was taking its toll.

He breathed a sigh of relief when Spotted Horse finally turned and rode back down the ridge. Survival was going to be hard enough under these conditions without human enemies to contend with.

Runs with the Wind watched until he was well out of sight before speaking. He didn't want his friend to make any sudden movement that might draw attention to them.

"Jeremy, did you see him?"

Jeremy sat bolt upright, frantically searching for his club, "What, where is he?"

"He's gone."

"Was it just one?"

"One what?"

"Wolf."

"It wasn't a wolf, it was worse, it was Spotted Horse again."

"What do you think he wanted?"

"Probably to make sure we were dead. Anyway he just sat up there looking for awhile and then left."

"He probably thought we were still over by those rocks."

"I think that's why he didn't see us."

"Do you think there are others out looking too?"

"Yes, but he will keep them as far away from here as he can. We will have to make it home on our own."

"We'll be ok," Jeremy said testing the pain in his wrist.

"How is your arm?"

"It's pretty sore, but everything works," he said continuing to flex his fingers, "What we need to do is start thinking about a way to get home."

"We won't get far as long a I can't walk," Runs with the Wind said looking down at his splinted leg.

"We'll make you a pair of crutches. It will be awkward at first, but you'll get used to them in no time. Carrying all this other stuff is going to be the hard part."

"We may have to leave some of the meat behind.

"You're probably right. There seems to be some small trees along the creek that didn't get burnt, I can use a couple of them to make a small travois with the buffalo skins and carry enough to last quite awhile."

"We will need to travel along the creek toward the rising sun for a while until it meets the river, then we can follow it north."

"Is it a long way around?"

It's farther than going straight to the village but we need to stay near water."

"Well," Jeremy said pulling himself to his feet, "we're not getting anywhere talking about it, I'll get started on that travois."

As he turned to walk along the creek in search of just the right size and shape poles to make the travois out of, the buffalo calf followed along constantly nudging him or rubbing his shaggy muzzle up and down his arm. The calf was a nuisance at times, but a comfort to have around at others. He placed a hand on it's wooly head and was surprised that the calf accepted the gesture without hesitation.

The first pole was easily found and trimmed of excess limbs. Jeremy leaned it against a small bush so that it stood upright and would be easy to locate on the way back. To find a second such pole that matched the shape and size of the first one proved to be an entirely different matter. For the most part, everything was badly burned or not suited for his purpose.

Jeremy walked along the creek bed kicking an occasional pile of ashes as he went. They billowed into the air like small summer clouds clinging close to the ground. The buffalo calf continued to follow along, unable to make any sense of the action, yet being careful not to step on large piles of ash that seemed to contain the glowing embers. After covering nearly a quarter of a mile, he finally found a tree that was suitable for his purpose. He took out his skinning knife and began the slow process of cutting it down. Hacking savagely at the base of the tree for several minutes produced very little in the way of results.

What he needed was more force behind the impact of the blade. Even though the tree was no bigger around than his arm at it's biggest point, it was still becoming quite a chore. Searching through the ashes on the ground, he found a rock along the creek that was about the same size as his fist. Using the rock as a hammer on the back side of his knife, made the blade bite much deeper into the wood. After a few more minutes of hacking the wood chips began to pile up and the tree was beginning to look as though it had been attacked by a beaver with broken teeth.

When the small tree finally toppled, Jeremy began to trim the limbs off using the same method of hammering the knife blade through each of them with the stone.

With that finished he started dragging the pole back toward their temporary campsite. Stopping along the way to collect the first pole he had found, it soon became obvious that dragging both of them was quite a bit harder, and when he considered loading them with the two robes and cured meat, he was sure it would be to heavy for him to drag very far at all. Runs with the Wind would most likely be able to travel faster on makeshift crutches than he could, and it might take them weeks to get to the winter village.

"I got the poles," Jeremy said dropping them to the ground near his friend, "but I'm not sure how well this will work."

"Why not?"

"I think it's going to be to heavy to drag very far," Jeremy said looking at the pile of dried meat that would weigh over a hundred pounds by itself. The meat would have weighed much less if they had taken the time to dry it properly, but time was working against them.

"Maybe there's another way."

"What other way, a shorter way home?" Jeremy asked hoping he wouldn't have to drag the contraption so far.

"Not a shorter way home, but maybe our young friend can help."

"The buffalo? He'll go crazy if we strap a travois to him."

"He might, but it's worth a try, otherwise you are going to be dragging it a long ways."

"I guess you're right, breaking a buffalo calf to harness probably would be easier than dragging this thing all the way back by myself."

"Who knows, maybe the spirits have put him here to help us. My father taught me never to question such things, just to accept them and use them to my best advantage."

"We had better get started, I might be able to find enough wood around here to keep a fire going tonight but tomorrow we need to move on. If we don't find a place with more firewood that isn't already burnt we'll freeze soon."

As if to accent his words tiny snowflakes started drifting to the ground all around them. A warning of what was to come in the next few hours.

"I better gather that wood first," Jeremy said noticing for the first time how heavy the clouds had become.

He had been so busy with his work that he hadn't noticed the thin white clouds becoming thicker and darker as the day wore on. He hadn't noticed the slight drop in temperature as he labored to cut down the tree, or drag the poles back to camp. Such an oversight could prove to be dangerous and he made a mental note to take a minute now and then to check his surroundings and the weather conditions coming their way.

So far they had been lucky. The weather had stayed warm for this time of year and there were no high winds. At times strong winds would blow out of the north piling the clouds up against the mountains and causing heavy snow to fall in the foothills in blizzards that would last for several days at a time. Anything over a few inches of snow would make traveling almost impossible.

Chapter Fourteen

Antelope and Spotted Horse rode along in silence studying the ground for any sign that someone had passed. Fresh ashes covered everything making it impossible to tell if anyone had gone through before the fire, but any tracks made after the fire would be clear and easy to find. They rode south for several miles, staying well to the west of the outcropping where Spotted Horse had last seen the boys, and made their way to the edge of the burn.

Antelope pulled his horse to an abrupt stop well inside the outer edge of the fire. "Two horses, headed east, moving fairly fast."

"That would be Red Fox and Coyote Track," Spotted Horse said, "They have gone on to meet the others."

Spotted Horse was not concerned about what Antelope might see anywhere around here, because the boys were last seen well to the north and would have no reason to travel south.

"We can look around here, or follow them and see what the others found."

There was no use back tracking the two riders because Antelope was pretty sure they had found nothing this far south, and it was far more important that he keep an eye on Spotted Horse. He wanted to be present if the man made even the simplest slip that might help find his nephews. It was going to be hard, not to let his true feelings overpower the false show of trust he had to display in order to maintain the charade.

If Spotted Horse had any idea how much Antelope knew it would be disastrous, and the boys would have no hope of being found. Without a word he turned his horse to follow those who had already passed. "Best to look to the future," he thought to himself as he rode through the endless ashes that seemed to be helping Spotted Horse hide his nephews, "for the past would be of no help to him in this matter.

Small grey clouds billowed around his horses feet as they moved through the burned out countryside. To the south, the unburned grass, even though dead with winter, showed the only promise of life in the area. To the north there were only the ashes, and two young boys that needed his help desperately.

"I'll find them," he said under his breath, "after this many days out here they have surely left some sign of passage somewhere. I just have to find it."

No sooner had the words left his mouth, than the first tiny snowflakes began to drift to the ground. Small at first, darting along on the breeze, disappearing to nothing as they stuck to the bare skin on Antelope's arms and face. Within minutes however, the flakes became more numerous and larger, and Antelope stopped for a moment to put on his heavy elk skin cape to protect himself from the evening chill as well as the new threat of heavy snow.

The cape wasn't anything fancy, but it served the purpose well, and it was the first thing Thin Woman had made for him after their marriage many years ago. She had tanned the hide with the hair in place and trimmed the edges in straight lines, producing a large rectangle. She then trimmed a hole out of the middle for his head to go through.

Slipping it on, he folded the sides in close to his body and tied it in place with the braided leather belt Thin Woman had made just for that purpose.

It wasn't long before he realized the warmth of his heavy cape wouldn't be enough, with the snow coming harder all the time. It was beginning to stick where the ashes had cooled completely, leaving only an occasional spot where hot embers remained to hiss and steam in defiance of the snow. Soon even those places began to succumb to the relentless onslaught of frozen whiteness called winter, and the ground once again found a way to conceal any footprints that might lead Antelope in the right direction.

"Antelope, over here," Little Wolf called out of the snow storm.

"Yes," he replied trying not to act to surprised. This was the second time today he had been caught off guard and not only was it embarrassing it was extremely dangerous, "I see you."

"Did you find anything?"

"Not a single track."

"And we won't find any now that the snow is coming," Little Wolf said, "if they are alive, they're probably held up in some nice warm spot with a fire going."

"I hope so," Antelope said straining to see through the falling snow.

"We should find such a place for ourselves," Spotted Horse said, "it will be dark soon and we will find nothing in this storm anyway."

"We found a cave in the cliffs along the creek a ways back," Little Wolf volunteered.

"Was there any wood left to burn?" Antelope asked.

"Yes, the cave was outside the burn area. We thought maybe they were in there so we went to check it out."

"Then we should go. We would do no good for them if we freeze out here tonight, we can continue the search tomorrow."

Darkness was closing in when the cave came into view. All seven members of the search party were shivering cold and anxious to get a fire going. Little wolf staked out the horses in the most suitable shelter he could find for them, while Antelope took out his fire starting tools and began the process of heating their sanctuary. The rest of the men broke dead branches off of the trees and gathered driftwood until they had more than enough to last through the night.

The entrance to the cave was low enough that they almost had to crawl to get into it, and ten to twelve feet wide. To cut down on the heat loss and prevent the wind from blowing in on them they stacked the firewood in the entrance on both sides, forming a small doorway in the middle.

The physical activity of preparing for the night had warmed them from inside enough to stop the shivering and chattering of their teeth, and the small fire Antelope had going toward the back of the cave was bringing the inside temperature up nicely. All in all it was going to be a more comfortable night than any of them had anticipated.

With the preparations for the night taken care of, they settled around the fire chewing on dried meat and discussing the possibilities of finding the lost boys. Until this point Little Wolf's companions had remained fairly quiet. Red Feather and Otter both felt that because they were the youngest members of the search party, they should let the older men handle the situation and try to learn all they could. Now in the safety and warmth of the cave with their stomachs full, they too began to voice their thoughts.

"We found nothing," Otter said, "but one set of tracks in the ashes made by a lone wolf."

"That's more than we found, " replied Coyote Track.

"There was no sign of life at all," Red Fox added.

"Could they be farther south than this?" Little Wolf asked.

Antelope had been quietly tending his own thoughts on that subject, as well as trying to read the thoughts of Spotted Horse who's stone like expression never seemed to change.

"I think we have already come too far south," he said. Antelope didn't want to sound sure of it, yet he needed to convince the others he was right without using the hard facts he had to prove his conclusion. He could not mention the fact that Spotted Horse had seen the boys on the day of the stampede without coming this far south, or it might put him, Little Wolf, Otter, and Red Feather all in a very dangerous if not deadly situation.

"Maybe we should split up and ride north on different trails tomorrow," Red Feather said eagerly, feeling the suggestion had strong merit to it.

"With this fresh snow there will be no track, but we might be able to see the smoke if they have a fire going," Otter said showing no less enthusiasm than Red Feather.

Antelope watched for a change in Spotted Horse's expression which never came. Apparently Spotted Horse was so confident that they could not be found, he didn't care where the searchers looked. And what if the storm were to continue, the snow was starting to pile up fast, and at this rate would be halfway up to their knees by morning.

"No," he said, "we must stay together. In a snow storm

like this we would only end up looking for more lost people, we have to stay together in order to survive."

"Antelope is right," Spotted Horse said, "we will accomplish nothing if we're all looking for each other. Besides if someone gets lost in the burned area, there will be no firewood to keep you from freezing to death."

Once again Spotted Horse showed nothing but good judgement and concern for those around him, and it made Antelope wonder if Elk Talker had been totally honest with them, or if it had merely been a ploy to achieve his own goals to become medicine man.

"What do you think we should do Spotted Horse?" Antelope asked.

"I think that in the morning we should head straight north watching for smoke, if the weather allows us to see very far, and get these young boys back to the safety of the village before it gets much worse. Then if you feel there is still reason to continue the search I will come back with you myself and we will only have ourselves to worry about."

"I agree," Antelope said, "it would be wrong to risk the lives of so many to find two that may already be dead. Tomorrow we will return to the village."

Chapter Fifteen

With a good fire going and plenty of wood to last through the night, Jeremy began the process of breaking the young buffalo to pull the travois. The calf had no fear of his scent or his touch, so that part of it would be easy. Jeremy cut several long, thin strips of hide from one side of his buffalo robe and braided them into a short rope. The calf stood perfectly still as Jeremy petted him and wrapped the leather strap around his neck. Tying the loop securely he wrapped the other end around his hand several times to insure a good grip.

With a gentle tug, he started off to lead the buffalo out of camp. That was all it took. As the rope tightened around the calf's neck, panic set in. He snorted and struggled to take in another breath. The leather strap was shutting off his air and he bolted. Racing along blindly through the ashes dragging Jeremy head first at his side.

Jeremy struggled to hold on to the rope and regain control, but it was no use. The buffalo calf was much stronger, and he was being dragged far to fast to regain his feet. The ashes burned in his eyes and each time he tried to breath he seemed to get more ashes in his mouth than air. He opened his hand to release the rope and nothing happened. The way he had wrapped it around his hand now had it in a bind that wouldn't come undone. Now it was his turn to panic. He clawed at the leather strap with his free hand, but could do nothing. The harder he pulled the tighter it got. He could feel the bones in his hand being forced together and the fingers were already numb. He had to try for the knot at the calf's neck. Grabbing the leather rope with his left hand, he pulled himself forward enough to give a little slack. Reaching hand over hand he got his right hand ahead of the left and tried to get another hold on the rope. His fingers were numb and wouldn't lock tight enough to hold, but the slack in the rope was loosening the wraps around his hand.

He pulled himself forward by bending his arms and was able to get a hold of the leather with his teeth. Pulling viciously he jerked the end of the rope back through the loop that had made the knot. His hands came free and he rolled across the ground coming to a stop face down in the dirt. Little puffs of ash blossomed around his head with each labored breath and his body ached from the beating he had taken.

Slowly and painfully he got to his feet and looked around in the increasing darkness for the fire that would point his way back to camp. Trudging back across the open ground it was hard to believe the buffalo calf had dragged him so far in such a short amount of time. Physically, he wasn't hurt bad, but his hopes of leading the buffalo along were all but gone. It could take days, or even weeks to break him.

So lost in his thoughts as he walked along, he didn't notice the muffled sounds behind him nor did he see the creature that followed along in his path until he stopped abruptly at the fire and the calf bumped into him, nearly knocking him down again.

"He follows better than he leads. Maybe you should try leading him without a rope."

"That's fine with me, I don't want to do that again, but what if he runs away with all of our food?"

"To start out you can carry one robe and enough food to last us a few days, that way if he runs off and doesn't come back we can still survive."

The two boys spent the rest of the evening designing a method that could easily convert the smaller of the two buffalo robes into a pack for Jeremy, as well as cutting holes in the outer edges of the larger robe and making straps to tie it to the poles for a travois for the calf.

When they awoke the next morning the snow had stopped, leaving a solid white blanket over the ground that was several inches thick. The sky was still totally covered in clouds and fog lay heavy in the lower country along the creeks and between the ridges.

Both boys knew it was do or die on this crisp cold morning because even though food was not a problem, keeping warm would be. They would have to reach the village or be found soon if they were going to survive.

Runs with the Wind laced up the pack with several pounds of jerked meat inside while Jeremy put the travois together. Using the braided rope that had nearly gotten him dragged to his death the day before, he tied the two poles together so that they would lay along the calf's sides and ran the rest of the rope back to the first pole to create a dangling loop to go around the front of the buffalo high on his shoulder, yet low enough that the strain of the pull would not choke him.

Catching the calf was no problem, since he was always at Jeremy's heals, the hard part would be getting the loop over his head.

"Well here goes," Jeremy said as he led the calf into position.

"Pet him for awhile first, and talk in a low voice. It might help to keep him calm."

"And if it doesn't?"

"Make sure he's headed north, that way when he loses the travois at least it will be closer to the village than it is now."

"Good idea," Jeremy said swinging the travois around to the right direction. "Ok fella, let's try this again.

Standing next to the buffalo's head, Jeremy continued to pat him gently and talk in as soothing a tone as possible while he stooped to lift the ends of the travois poles. He had some difficulty getting them high enough to go over the calf's back, but when he did he stopped petting him long enough to grab the dangling loop with his left hand a drape it over the buffalo's head. The calf stood perfectly still as the loop settled into place. Jeremy used both hands to lower the travois poles into position on each side of the calf without any sudden movement. The young buffalo shuddered visibly as the weight was transferred from Jeremy to him, but remained where he was.

"So far, so good," Jeremy said shouldering his pack.

"We'll get started and you follow as fast as you can."

Jeremy began walking north and the calf started to follow. With his first step, the weight of the travois and the backward pull frightened the young buffalo once more. Lunging against the drag and kicking into thin air, the calf tried to rid himself of the unfamiliar contraption holding him back. He bunched his muscles and leaped forward, breaking into a dead run. The boys could only watch as one of their robes and most of their food disappeared in the fog.

"I should have put you on that thing," Jeremy said grinning at Runs with the Wind. "You would have been home in no time."

"I think I would rather walk, at least now I only have one broken leg."

This was the first time they had laughed in a long time and it felt good. No matter what happened to their supplies they were alive and headed home.

"Let me help you with the crutches," Jeremy said helping Runs with the Wind to his feet, "it could be a little tricky in the snow."

"At least we have a good trail to follow, he's headed right for camp."

"It's a good thing you had me get him pointed north, or all our stuff would be going over those high mountains to the west about now."

"How far do you think he'll get before that strap breaks?"

"It's hard to say, I've seen braided leather straps like that take a lot of punishment."

"If he gets all the way to the village someone will back track him. No one has ever seen a buffalo pulling a travois, their curiosity will force them to come."

Even as the boys continued this line of conversation they knew no help would come of it, but it gave them something other than their cold hands and feet to think about as they trudged through the snow.

Runs with the Wind was doing good with his crutches, though his best was still a very slow pace. By himself Jeremy could cover the ground several times faster, but there was no way he could leave his friend behind. Runs with the Wind couldn't carry a pack, and would therefore have no food or buffalo robe to keep him warm. The only way for them both to stay alive was to stay together. Besides they only had one set of fire making tools, and without Runs with the Wind, Jeremy knew he would freeze on the first night out.

With periodic rest stops, they covered about a mile in the first hour of traveling. Not bad under the circumstances, but they both knew it would be a long trip. At a good steady walk the distance could be covered in three days, but at the rate they were traveling two weeks would be closer to the amount of time required.

They continued to follow the buffalo's trail, and were amazed that the travois was still holding together. They had found only a few pieces of dried meat laying in the churned up snow, in the wake of the miniature stampede, and had eaten them as they walked along.

Suddenly the silence was broken by a familiar bleating sound. Straining to see through the fog the boys made out the shape of the young buffalo headed back in their direction. He seemed bewildered and resigned to dragging the travois and didn't waste any more of his energy trying to kick at it. The only emotion he really showed was relief at the sight of his new companions.

He broke into a ragged trot, undaunted by the resistance of the travois, and came to a stop only when the boys were within a few feet of him.

"Good boy," Jeremy said throwing his arms around the calf's neck, "I knew you would come back."

"Let's keep walking Jeremy, we need to see if he will follow us."

Jeremy led the buffalo in a small half circle so the travois wouldn't bind up as the calf turned, and sure enough he followed right on his heels. When they were headed north again Jeremy came to a stop to wait for Runs with the Wind to catch up. He rubbed the calf's neck and scratched behind his ears. To return the show of affection the young buffalo licked Jeremy on the face with a tongue as rough as sandpaper, a gesture Jeremy could have done without, yet it was good to know there was a bond between them.

"Did you see how easily he pulls it?" Jeremy asked almost as proud as a father watching his sons first steps. "He could pull twice that much weight."

"We don't have anything else to put on it but the pack you are carrying, and I don't think we should risk all of our food."

"I'm not thinking about my pack, I was thinking about you."

"You want me to ride on it? He's not even broke yet."

"You'll be fine, besides he's to tired to run much farther."

"What if he's not?"

"Then you can roll off in the snow, or hang on until he stops, and I will catch up as soon as I can, but we have to do something to travel faster."

"Then hold his head until I get on good."

Jeremy stopped in front of the buffalo calf and started scratching behind his ears again. The calf paid no attention as Runs with the Wind settled onto the travois and got a firm grip on the leather straps that held the robe in place.

"I'm ready," he said wondering if he really was.

"Ok, let's go," Jeremy said, backing up the first few steps to keep an eye on the buffalo's reaction.

The calf leaned against the leather strap and realized immediately that something was different. Turning his shaggy head to look back, he saw Runs with the Wind sitting on the pack of dried meat with his teeth clenched and his knuckles turning white from the pressure of squeezing the leather straps. The calf looked back toward Jeremy who was now several steps ahead and leaped against the make shift harness. The travois jerked forward and the calf fell into a steady walk at Jeremy's heels.

Runs with the Wind unclenched his teeth but maintained his solid grip on the leather straps not yet convinced that everything was alright.

Jeremy glanced over his shoulder to make sure everything was alright, and began to walk faster. In the next hour they covered nearly four times the distance they had previously gone, and satisfied they were making good progress, Jeremy stopped to let the buffalo calf rest.

As Jeremy laid his pack on the ground and sat down on it to rest, Runs with the Wind spoke in a serious tone Jeremy had never heard him use before.

"My brother, do you know your spirit animal?"

"My what?"

"Your spirit animal, everyone has one."

"If I have one, I sure don't know what it is."

"Then when you start walking again I think you should look behind you, and you will see it as clearly as I do."

"I don't think..."

"Don't scoff at your spirit animal big brother, or he may abandon you. We all need help sometimes, and your spirit animal can give you that help if you let him. Sometimes in the real world, sometimes in your visions. That is the way of the spirits, do not question it, accept it, and praise them for their help."

Jeremy knew he was serious, and at times it was not going to be easy being the blood brother to the son of a medicine man. He wasn't at all sure that the buffalo was his spirit animal or how to go about praising the spirits for him if he was, but just to be safe...

"Hear me oh Great Creator of all things. I am a young man who wishes to thank you for my spirit animal, and all of his help. I thank you for watching over us and helping us to get back home. Amen."

"Amen, what does that mean?"

"It means I ain't taking any chances."

Chapter Sixteen

Daylight was slow in coming to the small cave where the search party had weathered out the storm. Outside, snow and ice covered everything, making it impossible to distinguish even the most used trails in the area. Fog had settled into the valley reducing visability to not more than a few yards in any direction.

Antelope and Spotted Horse, being the most experienced warriors, led the way as they started north. When they reached the top of the first ridge, they had ascended above the fog. The only visible points as far as the eye could see, were just the tops of the rolling, snow covered hills. Everything else was shrouded in an icy grey blanket called winter.

Ruling out the possibility of continuing the search on the way back to the village, Spotted Horse and Antelope both realized it would take all of their combined knowledge and experience to get the search party home safely.

Thick heavy clouds covered the entire sky only a few hundred feet above their heads, leaving them with a narrow range of vision all around. Everywhere they looked, all that was visible was the white of the snow covered hilltops, or the dingy grey of the fog below and the clouds above.

"We have stayed to long," Spotted Horse said, taking a look in all directions.

"You may be right," Antelope replied, "we must waste no time getting back."

"How can you find the way?" Little wolf interrupted, "with no sun or stars or visible landmarks to guide you?"

"We came to the cave from behind, which is that way," Spotted Horse said pointing west, "so we will go back that way until we hit the high mountains. We can follow them north until we reach the river of Little Beavers. It will lead us back to camp."

"I agree," said Antelope, "it is farther to go that way, but it would be the best way to keep from getting lost, and the mountains would provide more protection if the weather turns worse again."

Reluctantly Little Wolf, Red Feather, and Otter followed as the others led the way back to the mountains in the west. They knew they could not challenge the decision of their elders, nor could they find their way back to the village on their own. As much as they hated to abandon the search for their friends, it would be hopeless to strike out on their own.

The snow became deeper, and the temperature dropped steadily as they got closer to the high mountains. It began to pile up in drifts several feet deep in places, forcing them to make small detours to get around them. The valley bottoms were the worst for deep snow, because it blew off of the ridges to settle on the lower ground.

The mountains appeared suddenly in front of them as the fog lifted a little increasing their view. Antelope turned his horse to the north, and began to ride parallel to the high peaks that would lead them home. Spotted Horse reined his horse to a stop, peering through the gloom to the northeast.

"I would like to try once more to find them," he said, "if they are moving in this snow there will be sign."

"We must stay together," Antelope replied, "we have to think of the good of all before risking more lives on those that might already be lost."

"They are your nephews," he said in feigned protest. "Can you turn your back on them when they need you?"

Antelope felt a twinge of guilt as he made the only reply he could. "We have other young lives with us to consider now, their safety must come first."

Once again the smug look on Spotted Horse's face could not be seen as he led the party north. He was sure that he had

Antelope thoroughly convinced of his sincere attempt to locate the missing boys, and the early blizzard would make certain that any hope of their survival was gone.

Antelope had similar feelings about the chances of survival for the boys, but the pain of loss he felt was real, and not so easy to hide. For many years he had watched as Runs with the Wind grew, and it had been he himself, that had taught the boy most of his skills as a warrior and hunter. Runs with the Wind had shown a lot of promise as he neared manhood, as well as being a good friend to the old man, yet even though the feeling of guilt was almost more than he could bare, the duty to his people and their survival as a race would always come first.

The wind began to pick up, blowing from the north, as darkness fell on the search party that was only half way home. It was going to be another long cold night for the weary travelers, and searching out a cave in the darkness would be impossible with the heavy snow that had started falling. They were large flakes this time, almost as big as bird eggs, and laden with moisture. It was the kind of snow storm that would soak a persons clothing through in no time, robbing them of precious body heat. It, combined with the wind, could be a deadly situation, and Antelope started looking for any type of shelter that the landscape might offer.

What he found was a small, heavily wooded box canyon. Near the back of the canyon there was little wind, and the trees afforded ample shelter for the horses. In the bottom of the canyon was a small creek that had turned to solid ice. It led to the cliff at the back end of the box canyon, where the extremely cold temperatures and lack of sunshine had allowed the water to freeze, layer upon layer, forming a sheet of ice that resembled a waterfall frozen in time.

The warriors picketed their horses on the leeward side of the largest trees, where they could paw through the snow to find the small amount of dead grass that remained or to chew on the bark and small limbs of the trees. With that taken care of, they began to search out the best places to protect themselves from the weather.

It was Little Wolf who noticed the small opening on one side of the frozen water fall, and went to investigate. The hole was barely big enough to put his hand through, and he felt around to see how large the space was behind the ice. He could feel nothing, so he shoved his arm in as far as it would go. Still he could feel nothing, except that the air inside was warmer than the air outside. Drawing his arm back out of the hole, he put his face up to it.

He could feel a gentle rush of air against his face as it escaped from the hole. A fresh air supply could mean only one thing, behind the sheet of ice lay a small cavern that had another opening somewhere on the mountain. The air was warmed slightly as it passed through the tunnels under the earth to emerge through the small opening Little Wolf had found.

Digging through the snow, he found a good size rock, frozen to the ground. Banging on it with a stick, he was able to free the stone from the earth's icy grip. He picked up the rock and began to chip away at the ice around the opening, making it larger.

He worked slowly, taking care not to shatter the wall of ice. If it were to break and fall on him, it would be like getting caught in a landslide of sharp, broken rocks.

When the opening was finally large enough to wiggle through, he went over to the fire that Antelope had started.

"I need to use a flaming stick," Little Wolf said squatting by the fire to warm his hands.

"You are welcome to share my fire," Antelope said, "there is plenty of room here."

"Thank you, but I think I found a cave behind that, and I need a torch to see how big it is."

"Let us look," Antelope replied, also eager to be out of the biting wind. He grabbed a flaming stick for himself and handed one to Little Wolf as he said, "Maybe there is room for everyone."

The slight rush of air through the opening made it impossible to keep the sticks lit as they tried to pass them through the hole. Little Wolf had crawled inside, but could still see or feel nothing.

"Do not move around Little Wolf, it could be dangerous. Let me hand you some sticks and you can build a fire inside."

By now, several of the others had gathered around to see what was going on. They started gathering small sticks and twigs for the fire that was being built inside the ice cave. When the flames flickered to life, it illuminated the interior, casting a distorted shadow of Little Wolf against the wall of ice that covered the entrance of the cave.

Spotted Horse's breath caught in his throat when he saw the shadow. It wasn't Little Wolf's silhouette that he saw, it was Runs with the Wind's, complete with the twisted leg. He watched as the shadow pointed an accusing finger at him, and tried to convince himself that it was only his imagination.

An owl hooted, and flapped it's wings noisily as it flew through the air to pass in front of the cave. This was not a good sign at all. Spotted Horse was sure the spirits were angry with him for what he had done, and were warning him of impending doom should he decide to seek the refuge of the cave.

"Come in," Little Wolf urged, "there is plenty of room."

One by one they passed their sleeping robes and weapons through the hole, along with some firewood, before climbing in. All but Spotted Horse who stood in the freezing weather staring at the numerous silhouettes that all resembled Runs with the Wind.

"Spotted Horse, come on in," Antelope said, "it's much warmer than out there."

"No, someone must stand guard while the others sleep."

"There is nothing to stand guard against. The storm has everyone and everything hiding from the cold just as we are."

"Maybe that is true, maybe not, but I'm not tired and I would feel a lot better knowing someone was standing guard."

"Very well, wake me later and I will take over."

"I will," Spotted Horse lied. He knew it was going to be a long cold night for him, sitting by his fire for warmth, but there was no way he was going in that cave when it's spirits were so actively against him.

Chapter Seventeen

Spotted Horse sat alert over his little fire, keeping a constant vigil for any spirits that might mean him harm. He had never had any face to face dealings with spirits of any kind, including on his vision quest, and he was not looking forward to dealing with them now.

Time after time through the night, he thought about that vision quest, and how the spirits had kept his vision away from him because they were apparently angry about the deer he had killed and feasted on while he was supposed to be fasting. Now with the slightest provocation they were out to punish him again. Spotted Horse preferred his enemies to be of this world, someone he could see and feel, someone he could defend himself against.

"Why are you punishing me?" he asked speaking softly to the heavens. "I did not raise a hand against him. It would have been easy, but I chose not to."

"Whoo, whoo," an owl called back as if to answer, sending a chill down his spine that could match anything the cold weather could produce.

The owl, being the messenger of ill fortune or even death, was the last thing Spotted Horse wanted to hear from on a night when the spirits were already angry with him, and he peered still deeper into the darkness seeking out the impending danger that he felt so close at hand.

His eyes burned and ached from the strain of staring into the darkness, and the smoke from his fire. He fought it as long as he could, but when they slid closed in that darkest part of the night, he let them stay that way for a moment to ease the pain.

He was almost asleep when he jerked his eyes open with a start. Something was wrong, but he couldn't tell exactly what. He tried to sit up, and felt the restraint of the cold, sharp metal edge of a knife at his throat. Rolling his eyes to the side, he could see Runs with the Wind kneeling by his head.

"You left us to die," he accused as he added more pressure to the knife.

"I didn't see you."

Spotted Horse hated to plead, but he hated the thought of dying on this cold miserable night even more.

"You saw us, and then you rode away to lead my father in another direction."

"No," he was becoming frantic now, "It must have been someone else."

"It was you, and it will be me that takes your miserable life into the next world to deal with the spirits you have dishonored so many times."

The quick thrust of the knife was to much for Spotted Horse and he jerked violently with a spasm of over tensed muscles. His eyes shot open, and even in the freezing chill of dawn, beads of sweat ran down his face. His heart was racing to the point of exploding out of his chest. His hand went to his throat feeling for blood, but there was none. It had been a dream, or a vision into the future, he couldn't tell which, he only knew he was glad it was over.

He was fully awake and the sun was almost up. The others would be coming out of the ice covered cave soon, and he put more wood on the coals to bring life back to the fire. He struggled with himself to be calm and fully in charge of his emotions when they emerged. He would show no weakness that might give him away. He planned to be their leader one day, and he would never be able to achieve his goals if he showed weakness or fear.

The storm had passed quickly in the night leaving only a couple inches of new snow on the ground. The wind had blown away the clouds without Spotted Horse noticing the change. He was startled to see the sun coming up in a clear blue sky where he had expected another day of heavy clouds and fog. Traveling would be a lot faster in clear weather and they would be able to make it back to the winter camp before dark without much trouble.

"Good morning my friend," Spotted Horse said being as cheerful and friendly as he possibly could. "It's a beautiful day, should we take the young men back to the village, or would you rather search for your nephews again today?"

"We are a long way from where they should be, and this snow storm may return, I think we should go back to the village and see if there is any word from them."

"Maybe you are right, I just hate to waste a good day without looking."

Antelope headed for his horse, followed by the rest of the search party. No matter how he looked at it, Elk Talkers story seemed to be far from the truth. Spotted Horse had been more than willing to help find the boys, he had even volunteered for the first search party. Now when everyone else had given up and wanted to get back to the warmth and safety of their lodges, it was Spotted Horse who once again wanted to resume the search. But why would Elk Talker make up such a lie about him. Night Hawk had already accepted him as an apprentice, so what would he have to gain from such a lie, unless he didn't want Spotted Horse to become chief... He would have to speak to Night Hawk again before the council took up this matter.

Chapter Eighteen

Traveling was much easier now that the buffalo calf was pulling the travois with Runs with the Wind on it. They covered a lot more ground than they had ever expected to, and by the end of the first day of travel it became apparent that they would be able to reach the village much sooner than they had thought.

They stopped to spend the night in a small grove of trees only a few miles east of the ice cave where the search party was spending the night. Had they known, two hours of walking due west would have let them find the search party. As it was, they spent the night among the trees in a small bowl made by pushing the snow away and piling it up on all sides. It wasn't as comfortable as sleeping in a warm dry cave, but it did afford them some shelter from the wind and blowing snow.

The next morning, the buffalo calf was not so willing to be strapped into the harness and it took Jeremy several attempts to get him into the right position. Once the travois was back in place, the calf kicked and bucked a few times before settling down to the inevitable chore of pulling it all day. Runs with the Wind settled into position and with the first few steps it was obvious the calf's muscles were stiff and sore from the unaccustomed work of the day before.

"Jeremy, stop here," Runs with the Wind said, as he rolled off of the travois.

"What's the matter?"

"It's to heavy for him to pull another day."

"But the weather is clear this morning, we need to keep moving."

"Maybe we could lighten the load."

"Do you really want to throw away all that meat?"

"We don't have to throw it away, we can bury it in the snow, and you can come back for it later if there is a need."

"Won't it ruin?"

"Not as long as the snow lasts, or the wolves don't find it. You can carry enough in your pack to get us back to the village."

"How long will that take?"

"Today maybe, tomorrow for sure."

"Good, let's unload it and get started," Jeremy said as he unlaced the pack that he had loaded only minutes before. "I didn't realize how much meat we had."

"I think our friend will be much happier now," Runs with the Wind said, scraping out a place in the snow to pile the meat.

When the last of the meat was buried, Runs with the Wind climbed back on the travois, and they started off again, traveling faster than ever. The buffalo calf had no trouble pulling the travois after the meat was left behind.

As the rate of travel increased, so did the roughness of the ride. Small rocks in the path would jolt him around occasionally bumping his broken leg on one of the poles that made up the travois. No longer were there sharp, shooting pains in his leg, but a dull throb that stayed with him constantly.

Finding their way was also much easier now that the sky had cleared. When they crossed the higher ground, Jeremy could easily pick out the high snow covered peak that towered over their cabin. The winter camp lay to the southeast of that same peak, so with a little adjustment to their direction of travel, Runs with the Wind soon had them on a direct route to their destination.

Two hours into their morning travel, they came to a high ridge top, overlooking a long narrow valley that ran from east to west, directly in their path. The north and south sides of the valley were both heavily wooded with scrub oak and thick brush. The foot deep snow made it impossible to find or follow any path that might lead them safely down the steep slope that ended abruptly at a wide stream running through the bottom.

"What's the matter?" Runs with the Wind asked, straining to see around the buffalo.

"I can't find a good trail."

"Just go slow, and work your way through the brush, we'll make our own trail."

Jeremy started down the hillside, cautiously finding the widest places between the trees. Frequent turns to the right or left made it hard for the buffalo calf to follow with the travois in tow. Several times it got hung up on a small tree or bush and Jeremy had to pull it free or swing it to the side so it would clear. It was on one of these occasions, when the slope was particularly steep, that the calf leaned hard against the harness at the exact moment the travois came loose from the snag. The surge of power, combined with the weight of the travois pushing from behind, sent the buffalo calf scrambling down the hill trying to maintain his footing.

Faster and faster he ran down the slope, trying desperately to outrun the wildly bouncing travois that continually forced him onward. Lowering his head, he plowed through the brush, deftly dodging the larger trees as he went. Runs with the Wind was not so lucky. Time after time he would slam into a tree trunk scraping the hide off of his knuckles or banging his head with a force that caused lights to explode in his eyes.

Frantically he tried to protect his injured leg, and when they reached a clearing near the bottom of the slope, he rolled free of the runaway travois, to land in the soft, knee deep snow. He rolled over twice and made a gentle splash as he landed head first in the icy water.

The instant shock of falling into the near freezing stream made Runs with the Wind forget about the aches and pains of his tormented body and he scrambled to the far bank.

Thirty yards away, the buffalo calf stood calmly catching his breath as if nothing had happened. Jeremy came running down the slope and stopped to step gingerly from rock to rock, crossing the stream without so much as getting his feet wet.

"Are you all right?"

"N-n-no I'm not," Runs with the Wind said through chattering teeth. "He nearly killed me."

"Just sit still, I'll get you a robe and we'll get a fire going in no time."

Jeremy unharnessed the calf and removed the larger piece of buffalo robe from the travois. Draping it around Runs with the Wind's shoulders, he hurried into the brush to gather twigs and bark to make a fire.

He carefully sprinkled the powder from one of his two remaining cartridges on the tinder and set to work with the fire bow. Several times now, he had made fires using this method and was becoming quite proficient. What took several minutes, seemed like several hours to Runs with the Wind, who eagerly awaited the first crackling of the tiny flames.

Soon Runs with the Wind stripped out of his buckskins, which were showing signs of freezing along the fringes, and sat huddled in the robe, next to a roaring fire. This too created a problem, because as the heat from the fire melted the surrounding snow, the buffalo robe began to get wet.

He was trying to figure out a way to sit close enough to the fire and not get wet from the melting snow, when Jeremy came back out of the brush carrying several limbs of an evergreen tree. He spread them on the snow forming a thick mat near the fire.

"Sit on these, it'll help keep you dry."

"You learn fast, big brother."

"Pa showed me this, I've fallen in the creek a time or two in cold weather myself. Let's just get your cloths dry so we can try it again, we still have a long way to go."

Chapter Nineteen

As the search party emerged from the box canyon where they had spent the night, familiar landmarks immediately came into view, pointing the way home. Antelope and Spotted Horse led the way, discussing the possible locations that might be hiding the boys or possibly their bodies.

"If they are alive," Spotted Horse said, "we should be able to see the smoke of their camp fire on such a clear day."

"And if they are dead," Antelope replied dryly, "the snow will hide their bodies until spring thaw."

"You can't think about that," Spotted Horse feigned sincerity, "we'll find them."

The day dragged by slowly for Antelope as they trudged their way homeward through the snow. His eyes continually searched the horizon to no avail, as his hopes for ever finding the boys waned with each passing step.

He was too caught up in his own thoughts to notice the growing confidence in Spotted Horse. The closer they got to the winter camp, the better his chances of successful revenge without implication became.

The villagers dropped what they were doing at the first sight of the returning search party and ran out into the open plains, through knee deep snow, to greet them and learn of any news they might have. Nearly everyone went, with the exception of Night Hawk and Standing Bear, who were sitting just inside Night Hawk's lodge.

"Are you not going to see what they found?" Standing Bear asked.

"I think they found nothing," Night Hawk replied, "the spirits told me in my vision that my sons would return with the buffalo. Do you see any buffalo?"

"No," replied Standing Bear, pulling his head back from the opening.

"Then you will not see my sons either."

"Are you not eager to hear if they found anything at all?"

"Antelope will come directly here to speak to me about it, I would rather talk in the privacy of my lodge where he can speak freely."

Standing Bear sat impatiently waiting for what seemed to be hours as the scouting party answered the questions of those who had stayed behind. He knew Night Hawk's faith in the spirits was stronger than most people, but found it hard to believe that it could be stronger than a fathers concern over his sons. It was apparent that Night Hawk had resigned himself to the fact that he would see his sons when the buffalo returned, and not before. He had braced himself for a long winter of waiting, and was not going to let his emotions out of check every time someone rode into the village.

Antelope climbed off of his horse in front of Night Hawk's lodge, and hesitated before going in. His heart was heavy with the news, or more directly, the lack of news that he had to report.

"Antelope."

The sound of his name startled him as he realized he had been standing by the entrance to long, lost in his thoughts.

"Are you coming in, or do you plan to stand out there in the snow all day?"

"I was trying to decide how to tell you I have no good news to report," Antelope said stooping to pass through the entrance.

"I know you did not find my sons, but what of this other matter you were looking into? Did Spotted Horse reveal anything that the council should know?"

"No, he tried as hard as the rest of us to locate the boys. When the snow storm became dangerous, it was me who called an end to the search. I felt it would be foolish to risk the lives of several more young men, when there was nothing to be found but drifting snow."

"The counsel will discuss this matter tomorrow, after you have all had a chance to rest. Whether you found the boys or not we must proceed, treachery among us can not be over looked."

"Are you sure there was treachery on the day of the hunt?" Antelope asked, looking into the face of his chief, "or was the treachery in our own camp?"

"What are you saying?" Standing Bear asked, "We know all we need to, Elk Talker has told us everything."

"What if he was lying?"

Antelope shifted his position on the floor of the lodge, trying to ease closer to the warmth of the fire. He had not expected the cold resistance of his chief to accept the fact that Spotted Horse might not be as bad as Elk Talker had said.

"What reason would Elk Talker have for lying about such a thing?"

Standing Bear's question was short and to the point, Antelope knew his answer must be formed along the same lines to have any effect.

"Maybe Elk Talker has reasons of his own for not wanting Spotted Horse to become Chief someday. If so, who would be a better ally to help prevent that from happening than the chief and the medicine man. Remember Elk Talker already has what he wanted."

"This is true," Night Hawk said, "we need some kind of proof. To banish a man from his people on the word of one whom we didn't trust in the first place would be no better than what Elk Talker has accused Spotted Horse of."

Standing Bear's anger rose, more at the situation than at the man who was pointing it out to him. "What proof do you need? We know he wants control of our village. We know he hates Night Hawk and his sons, and we have Elk Talker's word about what happened."

"Yes," Antelope said, "we do, but we have to remember, Elk Talker also knew these things, before we had his word."

"This is an important matter," Standing Bear said as he rose from the fire to leave. "It is getting late and we should get some rest. Tomorrow the council will discuss it at the central fire, and anyone who has information will be welcome to speak."

"You're going to make this public?" Antelope asked. It was rare for the council to make such decisions with the entire village looking on.

"It is a matter that concerns everyone, and all should have a chance to say what they know. You are welcome to speak for Spotted Horse if that's what you feel is right, but tomorrow I have a feeling you will get the proof you seek."

Chapter Twenty

Little Wolf hated the duty he had been given early this morning. The council was meeting today at the central fire to discuss something of great importance to the entire village, and he had been selected as one of the four sentries to stand guard. This meant that he would have to ride a mile or so south of camp and watch for approaching enemies from a cold, secluded vantage point while the whole village discussed something so important that no one would talk about it before he and the other three scouts had gone their separate ways.

He felt cheated and alone. He had no idea what was going on that was so important that the council would make it public, but he was sure it was more exciting than sitting alone on the prairie watching the snow melt.

Back in the village, things were beginning to get underway, as some of the younger men built a large fire in the central pit. Interest began to build because there was a sense of an important event, ready to unfold in their midst. No one had been notified, due to the need to keep the reason secret until everyone was present. Standing Bear was not going to give anyone a chance to coerce witnesses or get their stories straight beforehand, and it would be impossible to do so at a public meeting.

The tribal elders sat at their places of honor on either side of Standing Bear. They waited patiently as the people crowded close to the fire so they could easily hear what was being said.

The last of the stragglers were making their way toward the crowd, when Standing Bear rose to address them.

"Everyone, we have a matter of grave importance to discuss here today." He turned to the elders and asked, "Are you ready?"

As one, they nodded in unison, maintaining the somber expressions that came with the dignity of the positions they held.

Turning back to the crowd, Standing Bear spoke loud enough for all to hear. "Elk Talker, would you come forward?"

"So this was it," Spotted Horse thought to himself, "Some kind of honor for the new apprentice of the medicine man. My plan is working well."

"Tell us Elk Talker, the story you told in Night Hawk's medicine lodge."

Now was the moment of truth, and Elk Talker wished that he had kept his mouth shut. No matter how it went today, things would never be the same again. If the council did not believe his story, he would be ostracized by his friends, and certainly by Spotted Horse, which would be devastating to him personally if Spotted Horse did indeed become chief one day. None of that mattered now as he stood in front of the entire village with everyone ready to hear what he had to say. He began slowly, and tried to avoid eye contact with the man who's life he was about to change forever.

"A few days ago, Night Hawk accepted me as an apprentice, something I have wanted for a long time. He had me stand on the edge of the village seeking approval from the spirits. All night as I prayed and chanted, my own spirit became heavy with a burden I could not carry. The next morning I told Standing Bear, Night Hawk, and Antelope, what Spotted Horse had told me about leaving Runs with the Wind and Jeremy to die after the buffalo stampede."

"Lies!" Spotted Horse shouted as he jumped to his feet. "I helped you to become apprentice for the medicine man, and now you lie about me?"

"Silence," Standing Bear commanded, "When he is finished, you will have a turn to speak."

Elk Talker began again, faster this time because the

adrenaline was flowing in his veins. "It is true, he told me he found them after the stampede, and left them for the spirits to decide their fate."

No one spoke as Elk Talker sat down, barely did they breath for fear of missing something. Spotted Horse puffed out his chest and walked to the fire pit to have his say. He wasn't going to let one weak hearted apprentice to the medicine man ruin the plan that he had been working on so long.

"My people, hear the truth. Who among you has searched harder for Runs with the Wind than I have. Who has spent more nights in the cold out on the plains than I have, searching for the lost boys. I don't know why Elk Talker lies, or what he has to gain by it, but surly my deeds speak for themselves."

Now a murmur went through the crowd as people were beginning to make up their minds. Clearly, the opinion was not unanimous as several arguments began to flare.

"Silence!" Standing Bear ordered to maintain control. "Everyone will be given an opportunity to speak."

Antelope was the next to come forward. He felt a duty to the husband of his sister and his nephews, but as far as he could see, there was no real evidence against Spotted Horse and it was up to him to say so.

"I would like to speak now," he said stepping up beside Spotted Horse. "I can see no clear answer in this matter. We have Elk Talker's word for what happened on that day, and I have never known him to lie, but what Spotted Horse says is also true. I have been with him searching for the boys, and we did everything we could to find them. He tried to hide nothing from us, and was the last to quit looking. What Elk Talker says is convincing, but we have no proof that it is true. I say...."

Suddenly the crowd turned it's attention to the sound of thundering hooves as a lone rider raced through camp toward the central fire. Their hearts raced and their pulses quickened as they realized the rider coming through the snow at breakneck speed was Little Wolf who was supposed to be on sentry duty to the south. Surly, trouble must be on the way.

"What is it?" Standing Bear shouted trying to be heard above the crowd.

"From the south," he gasped trying to catch his breath, "come see."

"What is it?" Standing Bear asked again trying to exert his authority.

"You'll have to come see it, you wouldn't believe me if I told you."

With that Little Wolf rode back to the south edge of the village where he climbed off of his horse and waited with a growing crowd of curious onlookers.

Chapter Twenty One

"I don't see anything," Standing Bear said, staring out over the rolling white plains.

"You will," Little Wolf said, barely able to contain his excitement. "It should be coming over the hill any time now."

"What should be coming over the hill?" Night Hawk asked.

"I told you, you wouldn't believe me unless you see it yourself."

A buzz went through the crowd as they anticipated what could have Little Wolf so excited that he would dare to speak to the chief and the medicine man without showing the respect that their positions demanded. Almost anything was expected to come over the rise, and the buzzing conversation became louder as the anticipation of the surprise grew stronger.

Silence fell over the crowd as the little caravan came into view. They had about a hundred yards left to travel but no one moved to greet them.

Jeremy led the way, wrapped in a heavy buffalo robe. He was followed closely by a young buffalo pulling a travois, with Runs with the Wind sitting proudly perched on his royal transportation.

Quail started to rush forward, but a firm hand on her

shoulder stopped her in her tracks.

"Do not interfere," Night Hawk said, "this is the work of the spirits, and not to be interrupted by people."

"It is as you said it would be!" Elk Talker exclaimed, "They have returned with the buffalo."

"Yes, but even I thought that meant they wouldn't return until spring."

"If it is a spirit thing, then why is it not Grand Father Buffalo that is helping them? He could have easily carried both of them home."

"Do not question the ways of the spirits Elk Talker. All things in life are connected, the boys are young, so the buffalo is young. The spirits would not do it for them, but simply help them do it for themselves."

As the boys reached the crowd Spotted Horse stepped forward to be the first to greet them. More than ever, he had to make a show of happiness and relief at the boys return, to help persuade the people that Elk Talker had lied.

Jeremy loosened the straps that held the travois in place and let the poles fall to the ground. He started walking back to help Runs with the Wind to his feet, when Spotted Horse ran forward almost bumping into them before he could stop.

"My brothers, I praise the spirits for your return." But the false show of emotion fell on deaf ears as Jeremy turned to face him.

Familiar with the customs, Runs with the Wind would have been more diplomatic in his reaction, Jeremy however settled for planting a well aimed fist squarely on Spotted Horse's nose, sending him flat on his back in the snow.

In shock and disbelief Spotted Horse scrambled to his feet, pulling a razor sharp knife out of his sheath as he came up. Stepping forward he slashed Jeremy across the arm as the younger boy tried to dodge the blow. It was a shallow cut, but it made the adrenalin shoot through his veins when he realized that for the first time ever, he was in a fight that could cost him his life. He jumped back again, and the knife slashed harmlessly through the air.

Spotted Horse held his weapon low and to the side as he crouched to come in for what he thought would be the final thrust that would end the life of the white intruder.

The unexpected crack of wood against bone sounded

like a gun shot, and Spotted Horse looked from his injured arm which no longer held a knife, to Runs with the Wind who was taking another swing with one of the heavy crutches that Jeremy had made for him. The second blow caught him above the right ear, causing thunder to explode in his head as he once again landed in a heap on the snow covered ground.

Now it was Spotted Horse who found himself fighting for his life, not with one opponent, but two. Separately either one would be no match for him, but together they proved to be quite deadly. He had to separate them and finish one at a time. He grabbed the fallen knife from the snow in his left hand and came off of the ground like a wild animal. He charged straight into Jeremy, and the force of his momentum carried them both several paces before they landed on the ground with Spotted Horse on top. He raised the knife over his head to make one last thrust that would even the odds.

Until now the buffalo calf had done little more than side step the commotion that was taking place, but once again this strange creature that his mother had become was in danger, and he lashed out the only way he knew how. Kicking with both hind feet, he caught Spotted Horse in the ribs. Bones crunched as the sharp hooves repeatedly lashed out. Spotted Horse fell silently on his side gasping for breath, brought down by the very creature he thought had killed the boys days ago.

Time stood still for Spotted Horse as he lay crumpled in the snow. He could see the awe struck looks on the faces of the onlookers, though no one came to his aid. It was as though he was outside his body, watching the scene without emotion or feeling, and his blood soaked slowly into the half frozen snow.

The pain had been intense at first, until his mind could no longer tolerate it, then in a moment of mercy the spirits had removed him from his body. Spotted Horse realized he was on his way to the after life.

"No," he screamed the words in his head, but no sound came from the limp body lying on the ground. "I won't cross over this way, not at the hands of these two boys."

The spirits were listening, and whether they felt sympathy for the man, or simply wanted him to fulfill his destiny, they hurled his spirit back into the tangled mess of pain on the ground.

Rough hands picked him up from the snow and pain

erupted once more throughout his body as broken bones and torn muscle tissue shifted into unnatural positions. A silky blackness ebbed forward, pushing the pain aside until all was darkness and peacefully quite, but he knew that this time he was inside his tattered body, and he would recover in time and have his revenge.

"Bring him to the council fire," Standing Bear growled, "we will deal with him there."

Night Hawk headed straight toward his two sons, who stood unsteadily together in the snow, not sure what was going to happen next. Even Jeremy knew that this type of behavior was not tolerated in the village, but he had let his temper over ride his good judgement, and now they would both have to pay the consequences at the council fire.

"Are you two alright?" Night Hawk asked.

"We're fine," Jeremy said, "I'm sorry I caused so much trouble, but when he walked up to us so friendly and smug, I couldn't help it."

"It is understandable. We know most of the story already, but you two will have to speak in front of the council before judgement can be passed on Spotted Horse."

"You knew he left us to die out there?"

"We knew he left you, but we couldn't find out where," Night Hawk said, "Come, there are many stories to be told at the council fire today." Then looking down at his sons splinted leg he asked, "Can you make it alright, or do you need some help?"

"We made it this far," Runs with the Wind replied, "we can make it to the fire."

"Night Hawk walked along between the two boys constantly looking over his shoulder at the buffalo calf that timidly stayed at Jeremy's heals.

"How did you do that?" he finally asked.

"Him? It wasn't that hard."

"He thinks Jeremy is his mother," Runs with the Wind cut in. "He couldn't get rid of him if he tried."

Chapter Twenty Two

Standing Bear stood with his shoulders square and his back straight, facing the crowd across the council fire. Spotted Horse lay at his feet, in a half sitting position, where the warriors who had brought him to the fire had left him. A constant murmur filled the air as once again the people argued with each other. Not about whether Spotted Horse was guilty or not, this time they were trying to decide what his punishment should be.

Jeremy's reaction to Spotted Horse, when he first made it to camp, had removed any doubt that Elk Talker was telling the truth. Spotted Horse had regained consciousness and struggled to fight off the pain that surged through him with each breath he took. His pride refused to let any weakness show through. This was only a minor setback. Soon enough he would be well, and he could resume his plans to gain control of the village.

Standing Bear raised his hand, and immediate silence fell over the crowd that didn't want to miss a thing that might be said. Not much exciting usually happened in a winter camp once snow started to pile up, but this year was proving to be much different already.

"This council would hear from Runs with the Wind now," Standing Bear said.

Runs with the Wind hobbled forward on his homemade crutches. He was getting much better at walking with them, and his leg didn't hurt near as much as it had when it first broke. He circled around the fire and took his place next to the chief, facing his people. He begun to tell his story and then stopped to lay his crutches aside. He stood on his right leg, using his left only for balance. Like his father, he was an eloquent story teller, and to be done properly a story had to be told as much with the hands as with the mouth.

He explained his plan to ambush the buffalo as they escaped in great detail. He told about the unexpected stampede as he and Jeremy attempted to reach the safety of the cliffs, and how they had been caught up in the raging flood of buffalo that poured out over the land. His elaborate description of their race for life had everyone straining to hear every word as their hearts pounded and they imagined themselves caught up in the situation. He described the way Jeremy's horse had been knocked out from under him, and how he had made a desperate run for the rocks, only to be knocked to the ground under the thundering hooves several feet from his destination. He then told how his own attempt to reach the rock outcrop had ended short of safety when his leg broke as he leaped from his running horse. He described the pain and fear as the unstoppable onrush of buffalo seemed to go on for ever without end.

"And then there was nothing," he said, "only darkness, and we slept through the rest of the stampede because the spirits knew we could stand no more pain. When the spirits brought us back into the world the next day, I opened my eyes to see Spotted Horse looking down on us. I raised my arm and tried to sit up to ask for help, and he looked at me with a cruel, uncaring smile on his face, and then he rode off to lead my father in a different direction so he wouldn't find us. Then, two days later, after we started the prairie fire to fight off the wolves, he came back and watched us from the ridge for a while. We had moved to the creek, away from the rocks, and when he couldn't find us he rode off to the north. That was the last time we saw him, until today."

He stopped there, he had told them enough for now. The details of their survival and the trip home were a story to be told at a happier time when they could all enjoy it more. Anything else now would only distract the council from the matter at hand.

"Do you have anything to say for yourself?" Standing Bear asked glaring down at Spotted Horse.

"It was a thing of the spirits, my eyes were blinded to

them so the spirits could continue their work."

"Then how is it you told Elk Talker you left them to the whim of the spirits."

"He lies!"

"It is you who lies," Standing Bear said, "your treachery and deceit shame us all. I say you should be banished from the people for all time. How does the council of elders speak?"

One by one they nodded in agreement and Spotted Horse felt a loneliness and despair he had never known.

"So be it, you shall be removed from the people to wander alone for the rest of your life. If you are seen in our lands in the future, you will be considered an enemy."

"Wait," Night Hawk said.

"What does the medicine man have to say?"

"We cannot send him away in the condition he is in now. With winter here and the wounds he has suffered, it would be no better than what he did to my sons."

"Then he may remain until spring, when his wounds have healed and the snow is gone, he will be cast out with nothing. Until that time he will remain in this camp as a captive, with no freedoms."

Standing Bear stood firm on this point, and left no doubt that he wanted no more arguments. "Who would take this captive?"

"I would," said Coyote Track stepping forward.

"But, you were my friend," Spotted Horse said, unable to believe what was happening to him.

"Be quiet," Coyote Track snapped as he grabbed Spotted Horse's shirt. Sticking his face in Spotted Horse's, he whispered through gritted teeth, "You better go along with this, I'll keep you alive through the winter, someone else," and then he raised his voice so everyone could hear, "might tie you outside the lodge to fight with the camp dogs over the scraps."

The realization of his situation hit Spotted Horse like a stone between the eyes. Everything he had worked for was suddenly gone. He was a man without a people, only the soft hearted plea of the man he hated most had saved him from a harsh and cruel death.

"Remove him from the presence of the people," Standing Bear demanded of Coyote Track, "you can collect his possessions when you wish, a captive is not allowed to own things, and since he is your captive, his possessions are now yours."

Spotted Horse couldn't stand this final indignity and started to protest venomously until Coyote Track cuffed him across the face to remind him of his place. Helplessly he slumped back to the ground, and Coyote Track, with the help of Red Fox, dragged him back to the privacy of his lodge.

"We are brothers forever," Coyote Track said once they were inside, "we swore it as children, and I say it again. But you are going to have to go along with this until you are well, then we will decide what to do."

Spotted Horse nodded helplessly, to weak to do anything about the situation, and set his mind to the future, when he would be well and strong again. Things would be much different then.

Chapter Twenty Three

With Spotted Horse out of the way, and no longer a concern of the people, the attention turned exclusively to Runs with the Wind and Jeremy, and more pointedly to the young buffalo calf that constantly stayed at their heels.

"Tell us," Little Wolf asked the question on all of their minds, "what medicine did you use to tame the buffalo?"

"It's a secret," Jeremy said, and then he leaned over to Runs with the Wind and whispered, "Tell them what happened, but let them think there was some magic involved, it will make it more interesting for them, and more fun for us."

Taking the cue, a smile came over Runs with the Wind's face as he began to tell the story. The people liked nothing better than to listen to someone who could tell a story masterfully, and Runs with the Wind was swiftly becoming known as one of the best.

As the council fire died down, the villagers headed back to their lodges, still talking excitedly about the latest adventures that seemed to follow Runs with the Wind since he had become acquainted with his adopted brother Jeremy. No matter the circumstances, they always seemed to come out on top.

Just before dark, as the snow started falling once again, the villagers settled into the routine of the long winter months ahead. With the success of the late season hunts to fill their food storage supplies, and the excitement that followed, to give them something to talk about, it would not seem as long as some winters when they were less prepared.

The winter months passed by much as they always did, with the exception of an occasional mishap caused by a certain buffalo calf, as he wondered through the village in search of Jeremy and Runs with the Wind. These rare occurrences were easily forgiven as his presence there was seen as an omen of good fortune to come. Why else would the spirits send a buffalo to spend the winter in their camp.

When the snow finally melted off, and the first sprigs of green grass began to show themselves, the hunters became more and more restless for the taste of fresh meat and the thrill of the hunt. They started venturing farther and farther south in search of the first herds to begin the migration north.

Then on a cool spring morning a lone rider came racing into camp with news of a large herd, two days to the south. In no time the hunters had assembled and were on their way, followed by the butchering party. Not so many animals would be taken on this hunt as on the one in the fall because they knew more buffalo would follow, and the demand for a large food supply faded with the last of winter.

Coyote Track and Red Fox volunteered to stay behind to guard the camp with Standing Bear and Antelope, who was feeling a little under the weather these days. There was not much danger of being attacked this time of year because all of their enemies would be out trying to replenish their own food supplies rather than going on raiding trips to other camps that likely had little more than they did.

This time as Night Hawk led the hunting party, Runs with the Wind rode at his right and Jeremy rode on his left. No man alive was prouder of his sons than Night Hawk was at that moment. They had shown they were worthy of being called men, and could take care of themselves.

Night Hawk knew this was not going to be a normal hunt by any means, because directly behind Jeremy was the buffalo calf that always dogged his trail. No one was sure exactly how things were going to work out taking a buffalo along on a buffalo hunt, but it was going to be interesting whatever happened.

Quail had made a brightly beaded strap of leather that

the boys had attached around the calf's neck so he could be easily identified at a distance. It hung loosely, flopping back and forth as he walked, but it gave him plenty of room to grow. They all knew it would not last forever, but it would keep him from being shot this season. No one of this tribe or any other would shoot a buffalo wearing human clothing around it's neck.

The plan was to take enough buffalo to feed the people, and integrate the young calf back into a life with his own kind. It presented several problems, but the boys had an idea of how to accomplish both.

Once the herd was spotted, the plans were quickly laid. The hunters set up several ambush points along the route the buffalo were taking, while Jeremy and Runs with the Wind circled to the south on foot. All they took with them were their weapons, the buffalo robes they had taken from the calf's mother, and of coarse, the buffalo calf himself.

Slowly but surely they worked their way around the herd of grazing buffalo, careful to stay out of sight. Once they were in position, a gentle breeze from the north carried the scent of the herd back to them. With the first whiff of his fellow creatures the buffalo calf became confused. This was a familiar smell that beckoned to all his senses, yet his instincts told him to stay with this new creature that his mother had become. That was where his security was, his feeling of belonging.

Closer and closer they crept, moving into position directly behind the buffalo. An old cow turned to watch as they got near. She took a few tentative steps toward them, and sniffed the air for any sign of danger, finding none she called to the calf to coax him back into the herd. Actually she called to all three of them, because Jeremy and Runs with the Wind followed along disguised as smaller calves by using their robes to hide under.

The calf's answer surprised himself almost as much as it did the boys, and he trotted a few steps closer. He turned to look back and his companions were still following even though they lagged back.

The calf continued on until he stood nose to nose with the cow exchanging scents. It was good to have the strong odor of motherhood fill his nostrils again and he was compelled to follow her back into the herd. He stopped on the outskirts of the loosely bunched animals and looked back to see what was taking his mother so long.

Just then a shot rang out as Jeremy dropped a cow not twenty feet from him. An arrow whizzed by to bury itself in the lungs of yet another buffalo even closer. Confusion mixed with panic, as old memories flooded back to him. The boys stood up waving the robes and screaming at the top of their lungs. Instantly the herd was moving in the direction of the ambush and the calf was running with them. With the protective instincts of a mother with no calf of her own, the cow stayed close to the new arrival as they fled.

"Goodbye my friend," Jeremy said as he watched the calf disappear into the distance.

For Jeremy the hunt was over. He had taken a buffalo for the lodge of his adopted father, and with the one Runs with the Wind had taken there would be plenty of meat for them and Antelopes family both. It was the duty of the hunters to hunt not only for themselves, but also for those who stayed behind to guard the camp, and with Antelope being family the responsibility fell to them.

It had been a long winter for Jeremy and the loss of his new friend only added to the need to see his own family again. His mind was made up, when the butchering was done and the others headed back to camp, with Night Hawks permission he would head straight home from here. With any luck he would be there early tomorrow.

Chapter Twenty Four

A few hours after the hunting party left, Coyote Track and Red Fox gathered their horses, as well as Spotted Horse's pinto, and brought them to the lodge where their provisions were packed and ready to go.

Healed for the most part, Spotted Horse was still stiff and sore from the kicking he had received from the buffalo, but he was ready to go. It took more effort than he had hoped to swing to the back of his pony, but once there he felt almost like his old self.

"Where are you going?" Standing Bear demanded.

"We are leaving, and I am taking my captive with me," Coyote Track said with a sneer. "I'll be back for the rest of my things later."

"He doesn't look like a captive sitting on that horse."

"How I treat my captives is my business old man," Coyote Track snarled with a contempt that took Standing Bear by surprise. "Out of my way."

The three men rode away with the knowledge they would not be welcome back there, at least until after Standing Bear had crossed over into the land of the spirits.

"You know, we have no home now," Red Fox said.

"We will make our own home, and take what we want," Spotted Horse stated flatly, "but first I have another matter to settle with my young friends."

They rode away toward the east, where they could make a temporary camp to wait for Jeremy and Runs with the Wind to head back to Jeremy's family farm in the mountains. Waiting was not a problem for Spotted Horse, as he had been waiting a long time for this opportunity. Now he needed only to decide the best way to punish those who had ruined his life before taking theirs.

On the morning of the third day Red Fox spotted the boys on their way to the cabin.

"They are to the south and east of us. They must have headed straight home from the hunt. We'll have to hurry to catch them."

"Let us go, I have been waiting for this day a long time."

The three warriors raced across the rolling foothills in an effort to intercept the two boys before they reached their destination. They came to a high open meadow at the south end of the valley that Jeremy's family had homesteaded, and began to plan their ambush.

While searching for the best hiding places, the sharp eyes of Spotted Horse caught movement coming out of the trees. It was a young girl leading a small horse, not yet old enough to be ridden. Long blond hair hung down past her shoulders, shimmering in the sunlight.

"This must be the Little Sun Spirit that Runs with the Wind is so fond of," Spotted Horse said as an evil grin crossed his face. "I have a better idea, we'll make them suffer for a while before we kill them."

"What do you mean?" Red Fox asked.

"We'll take the girl, and kill them when they come after her. I'll keep her for myself until I tire of her and then later we can trade her for supplies somewhere else where no one knows her."

Like ghosts of the night, they melted into the scenery. Coyote Track crawled slowly through the wild flowers toward the trail that lead through the meadow until he was in position. Spotted Horse and Red Fox remained mounted where they were in the edge of the trees.

The first indication of trouble that Misty noticed was when Thunder jerked the lead rope out of her hand and bolted away. Still shocked by the actions of her horse, Misty never saw

Coyote Track come up out of the wild flowers and swing the heavy stick that landed a tremendous blow to the back of her head.

Slinging her limp body over his shoulder, Coyote Track headed back toward the horses.

"Hand her up to me," Spotted Horse sneered, "I want them to see her."

They didn't have long to wait, because it was then that Jeremy and Runs with the Wind came into view. They stopped abruptly when they saw the all too familiar figure sitting astride that huge unmistakable pinto.

"Spotted Horse," Runs with the Wind said almost under his breath.

"What do we do now Little Brother?"

"I'm not sure, but we're in for a fight."

Spotted Horse swung his pony around to face the boys making both of them catch their breath as they recognized Misty sitting in front of him on the horse.

"Now what?" Jeremy asked.

"We are going to have to take her back. I hope you know how to use that rifle."

"I can't shoot him like this, I might hit Misty."

"Then I'll take Spotted Horse, you even the odds."

Runs with the Wind let out a war cry and kicked his horse forward as he knocked an arrow in his bow. Jeremy pulled his rifle out of it's scabbard and followed at a run. His first shot caught Red Fox high in the chest and slumped him forward on his horse. He levered in another round and pulled down on Coyote Track. Click... a misfire, or possibly a dead round. Feverishly he worked the lever to put in another round as an arrow tore through his shoulder flipping him backwards off of his horse.

Coyote Track let go another arrow that took Runs with the Wind's horse through both lungs. Almost immediately Runs with the Wind knew his horse was going down, and he was barely able to kick free to keep the horse from rolling over the top of him.

Spotted Horse laughed as he kicked his horse and rode away. Runs with the Wind ran to where Jeremy's horse had ground hitched himself after losing his rider. He still had his bow and several arrows, so he ignored the rifle laying on the ground as he swung into the saddle.

A low groan from behind brought his attention back to his best friend and brother lying in the grass. He had thought Jeremy was dead, now he had a real problem. He couldn't leave him here, and he couldn't take up the chase he so desperately wanted to.

Climbing back down from the horse, he checked Jeremy's wound. It wouldn't be too serious if it was properly taken care of, but he didn't have time for that. He helped Jeremy into the saddle and quickly lashed his wrists to the saddle horn. Climbing up behind him Runs with the Wind snapped the arrow shaft off as close to the skin as he could. Jeremy grimaced with pain and gritted his teeth. With a quick jerk Runs with the Wind pulled the arrow the rest of the way through. Jeremy's eyes went wide, and then rolled back in his head as he passed out.

It was not far to the cabin, and at Runs with the Wind's constant urging, Renegade was able to cover the distance in no time at a dead run.

"What is the matter?" Cheryl shrieked as she burst through the cabin door.

"Jeremy's been shot, and they took Little Sun Spirit."

"Who took her?" Cheryl was frantic now.

"Spotted Horse."

"Who is Spotted Horse?" Cheryl screamed, becoming dragged deeper and deeper into a nightmare that just kept getting worse.

"I'll tell you about it later, now I must go after them."

He swung back onto Renegades back and left at a gallop before Cheryl could ask any more questions. He stopped to pick up Jeremy's rifle before picking up the trail. He wasn't sure how well he could shoot, because even though Jeremy had taught him how to use it, he had never actually fired it.

Not far down the trail he found Red Fox. Spotted Horse and Coyote Track had left him where he fell, unfeeling and uncaring. Now there were only two, but they were a deadly pair. It was going to take all the cunning and knowledge he had to finish this fight by himself. He rode in silence for several hours studying the trail, as he tried to figure out exactly where Spotted Horse was headed. He was deep in thought when Renegade stopped and fought to turn back. A growl from the tree over the trail ahead sent every nerve on edge.

It was to far for the cougar to leap, and Runs with the Wind let an arrow fly with the accuracy of a practiced hunter. The giant cat clung to the limb it was perched on to no avail. It was dead before it hit the ground.

Runs with the Wind circled around the cat and started on down the trail when an idea struck him. He took some of the greasy pemmican out of Jeremy's saddle bags and put it on a flat rock. He went to a cedar tree and pulled off a handful of the heavily scented leaves which he ground into the pemmican with a rock. He then took the strong smelling mixture and rubbed it all over Renegades nose.

The horse snorted and backed away. The odor was strong, and he couldn't smell anything else, which is exactly the result Runs with the Wind was looking for.

Taking Jeremy's half of the buffalo robe that was still tied behind the saddle, he rolled the cougar up inside. Unable to smell the danger, Renegade paid little attention to the familiar bundle as Runs with the Wind lifted it back into place. Now he had the idea and the means, all he needed was the place to make it work.

Spotted Horse was in no hurry, and Runs with the Wind knew he wanted to be caught. He wanted to put an end to this today. They were traveling a well used trail, and to follow would sooner or later lead to an ambush.

"Come on boy!" Runs with the Wind said as he swung Renegade off of the trail. "It's a little rougher, but it's shorter and faster, and we have to get ahead of them."

The sun was dropping in the west when Runs with the Wind saw them coming along the trail. Apparently Misty had been more of a problem than Spotted Horse wanted to deal with, or he just wanted his hands free for the final battle between the two of them. Either way Coyote Track was riding along behind him, and now it was he who had Misty on his horse.

Runs with the Wind set up his ambush along a narrow stretch of trail where it went around a steep bluff on the left and had a sheer cliff on the right. He had left Renegade tied in the brush far enough back so the other horses wouldn't get his scent. The wind was blowing in his face as he watched them approach.

They stopped and looked back before starting around the bluff. Spotted Horse grunted in disappointment that Runs with the Wind had not yet appeared on their back trail. He had expected immediate response once Jeremy had fallen.

Runs with the Wind let him pass unhurt and saved his first arrow for Coyote Track. The range was close, and the arrow made a dull thud as it took him off of his horse before he could make a sound.

Coyote track's grip on Misty pulled her to the ground with him, and she cried out in pain as she hit. Spotted Horse looked back over his shoulder to see what the commotion was, or he might have noticed the trip line across the trail before his horse stepped on it. From a tree directly overhead that was growing out of the bluff, a cougar left it's perch to land directly on the pinto's head. His trap had worked better than he had dared to hope, sending the horse into total panic. He didn't know or care that the cougar was already dead, he cared only about getting away. Ignoring the frantic commands of his rider, the pinto turned to flee and stepped into thin air.

Spotted Horse's screams echoed through the canyon as his most trusted war pony took him for one last ride.

"Little Sun Spirit," Runs with the Wind called, "are you alright?"

There was no answer, save a low moan coming from the direction in which he had last seen her. "He ran to her side and relief flooded through his entire being, as he noticed the shallow breathing.

"It's over now, you won't have to worry about him again," he said, gently lifting her head as he checked her over for any wounds she might have sustained.

Her only response was a blank stare. She appeared not to be seriously injured, but she did have a tremendous amount of bruises, and her mind seemed reluctant to deal with the traumatic experience she had endured. Runs with the Wind helped her to her feet, and gently led her along the trail to the place where he had hidden the horse. When they reached the spot where Renegade was tied in the brush, Runs with the Wind looked at Misty in a new light. She was almost thirteen now, and for the first time he realized that his Little Sun Spirit was growing up, maybe too fast. He didn't know how long it would take for her to snap out of it and return to her old self, but she was young, and her experience had not been as bad as some that he had seen others recover from, however it still tore at his heart to see her standing there like that.

Misty clung desperately to the remnants of her torn and tattered blouse, trying to hold together the little bit of it that remained. Her head reeled as uncontrollable thoughts raced through her mind. It was partly from the serious beatings she had received throughout the day, and partly from her mind's refusal to accept the things that had happened to her. Without speaking, she had followed Runs with the Wind through the trees to the secluded spot where they now stood and even though she wanted to speak, she seemed too confused to turn her thoughts into words.

With her head down, she stopped at the edge of the clearing, and stared at a large purple bruise on her right forearm. It was a curious thing. Painful and brightly colored as it was, surely she should have noticed it when she got dressed this morning.

"Sun Spirit, are you alright?"

The sound of her name, from the familiar voice of the one who had given it to her, slowly seeped into her consciousness dragging her back from her trance-like state to the chilling reality that she had endured over the last few hours. The danger was behind her now and the realization of it was overwhelming. Tears flowed freely down her blood stained cheeks as the memories came flooding back and she sobbed uncontrollably.

Early that morning she had been brutally hit over the head with some kind of club, and carried away by the savage renegade, Spotted Horse. Since that time she had been beaten on several occasions, and tied with rawhide strips that cut into her wrists without mercy.

After her abduction she had been conscious enough to witness parts of the running battle that followed. Once again in her mind she saw her brother Jeremy take an arrow in the chest as he galloped to her rescue. The force of the blow carried him out of the saddle and threw him to the ground, where he was lost from view, hidden by the very same flowers of early spring that had enticed her into the meadow in the first place.

Moments later she had seen Runs with the Wind and his horse both go down under a flurry of arrows, and had lost all hope of rescue. From that moment on everything seemed to be a vicious nightmare that she could not escape until her mind had finally refused to accept any more punishment. She had remained unconscious a good part of the day, and mostly incoherent the rest of the time.

Now that Runs with the Wind had somehow miraculously appeared to rescue her, the release from anxiety and pain was overwhelming. She had always been comfortable around Runs with the Wind, and had felt a closeness to him since their first meeting almost a year earlier.

"You're cold," Runs with the Wind said shrugging out of his buckskin shirt, "put this on."

She accepted the shirt with her left hand, while still clinging to the torn blouse with her right. Runs with the Wind turned back to the horse and began removing the hobbles from the front feet. Not so much because he was in a hurry, but to give Misty the privacy she felt she needed to change.

It was a strange custom of the white people that he did not fully understand, but was more than willing to go along with for her sake. Nudity was nothing new to him. For an entire family to live in a teepee together, there was no such thing as privacy, and he had learned no need for it. His first experience with the white man's need for privacy was when Jeremy had gone to stay with them at the Cheyenne winter village. That first night when his mother had slipped out of her doe skin dress to go to sleep, Jeremy had been taken completely by surprise. Even though he had averted his eyes almost immediately, Runs with the Wind had seen his embarrassment, and noticed the deep shade of red as his face took on the new color in the glow of the firelight.

Jeremy had spent the entire winter with them, and still wasn't extremely comfortable with the situation. So he knew that Misty must be feeling much the same way.

In the near darkness, she removed what was left of her blouse and pulled the buckskin shirt over her head. The leather still held the warmth from his body when she pulled it into place. As the shirt came over her head she could smell the leather, and the smoke of a hundred cooking fires and a faint musky scent that triggered a feeling deep within her that she didn't understand. The overall effect of it was comforting and therefor a welcome change.

After adjusting the shirt that was half again to large for her, she turned to face Runs with the Wind. He stood with his back to her, pretending to be busy with the saddle and sleeping roll that was tied on behind.

A year ago when they had first encountered him, he had been small for his age. She hadn't realized how much he had grown. Almost sixteen now, he was as tall as most men, with broad shoulders and copper colored skin stretched taunt over rippling muscles. As he turned to face her, she saw anew the sharply chiseled features of his face with high cheek bones and his ever present smile. If she had been able to choose anyone to come to her rescue, it would have been him.

"Jeremy!" she said, suddenly snapped out of her thoughts by the sight of his horse. She had been so concerned over her own predicament that she hadn't realized that Runs with the Wind was riding her brothers horse.

"Is he alright?"

"He's at the cabin, with your mother."

"But is he alright? I saw an arrow hit him in the chest and..."

"He'll be fine, the arrow hit high, here," he said indicating a place high in the left shoulder area. "He's going to hurt for awhile, but it will heal. That's why it took me so long to catch up to you. I had to take him home first."

He sensed her reaction even before it came, and stepped forward to catch her, as she sagged into his arms weeping uncontrollably.

"I, I was so, so scared," she managed to say between sobs. "I thought he was going to, to kill me."

"It's ok, he can't hurt you anymore."

For the best part of an hour they stood there, with her shaking in his arms and crying uncontrollably. Cramps began to rage in his arms and legs, but he dared not let go of her now. The pain in his limbs was nothing compared to the pain in his heart for what Spotted Horse had done to her because of him. His only regret was that Spotted Horse had died to quickly when his horse had leaped from the cliff trying to escape the trap he had set.

When the sobs finally subsided, Runs with the Wind climbed onto the horse and helped Misty on behind him. Slowly heading back down the trail toward home, it was soon apparent that the mental and physical strain had taken a tremendous toll.

Less than a mile from where he had rescued her, Runs with the Wind reined his horse off of the trail into a small clearing. "We'll stay here tonight," he said, swinging his leg over the horse's head and sliding deftly to the ground.

"I thought we were going home."

"Tomorrow, you need to rest, and the clouds keep hiding the moon making it hard to travel."

He helped Misty to the ground and untied the small roll of buffalo hide that she had been riding on behind the saddle. It wasn't much, only half of a hide that he and Jeremy had split last fall, but it would have to do. This would be their only protection from the dropping temperatures and the storm that was coming out of the north.

Already a few drops of rain were beginning to fall and the lightning was coming closer.

"I'll start a fire, you gather as much wood as you can. But stay close, I'll get enough to get us through the night when the fire gets going."

Runs with the Wind took out the fire starting tools that he always carried in a small pouch at his waist. Within seconds he found a small limb to tie the leather thong on to make a fire bow, and set to work.

Misty began gathering sticks and twigs in and around the edges of the clearing. They had been lucky to come upon such a good campsite in the dark. The trail ran along the bottom of a small canyon at this point with the clearing on one side and a tiny stream on the other. Scrub oak, still without the leaves that would come later in the spring, along with pinion pine and juniper trees allowed for ample wind protection on either side. At the back of the clearing a solid rock cliff rose like a giant wall for more than fifty feet. A small depression in the rock at the base of the cliff would allow them to avoid the brunt of the rain storm that was beginning to increase in intensity.

In a flash of lightning, Misty noticed a huge pine tree just a little way back up the trail. It was nearly four feet thick at the base and sixty feet tall. Lightning strike scars and burn marks showed from top to bottom and several dead limbs lay on the ground at it's base.

She drug the first limb back into camp and dropped it outside the depression where Runs with the Wind had a fire coming to life.

"Keep adding twigs to this and I'll get the rest before it gets wet," he said, before she could leave again.

Glad for the chance to relax, Misty sat down in the back

of the depression and leaned against the smooth rock. Here she could sit comfortably and feed sticks into the fire that was growing quite nicely.

Runs with the Wind returned with his second load of wood as a blinding flash of light lit up the sky. A resounding boom of thunder momentarily deafened them as a shower of sparks fell all around. The giant pine tree splintered and the top two thirds came crashing to the ground. Runs with the Wind leaped to the back of the cavelike depression pressing Misty to the wall to protect her with his own body.

Renegade, content to be ground hitched until now, felt the tingle of static electricity from the onset of the lightning strike. As parts of the tree exploded into the night he bolted in terror. His departure was almost soon enough to carry him out of harms way, but not quite. The end of one of the upper most branches caught him along the right hip, ripping a nasty gash halfway down his leg. The pain only served to intensify the horses desire to escape. His left front foot came down on the reins as they dragged the ground. His forward motion carried him along while his head was being pulled down between his front legs. Renegade clenched the bit in his teeth and strained his bowed neck muscles for all he was worth. The reins snapped and his head flew up to where he could again see where he was going. Again and again close lightning strikes and loud thunder forced the animal to continue in a panic stricken run.

Within the space of a few minutes the lightning storm passed over the canyon, leaving in it's wake a light drizzling rain and the distant sound of thunder.

Looking out into the clearing where the dead pine tree now lay shattered, Runs with the Wind said, "I think you have enough wood now, I'm going to see about Renegade."

"But he's gone," Misty said, "and I don't want to be alone out here."

"We need the horse, he probably didn't go far anyway."

"But..."

"I won't be gone long," he said, as he started down the trail at a steady trot wishing that he could believe what he had just told her.

Chapter Twenty Five

"Ma,aaa..." The word caught in Jeremy's throat, as he tried to set up in bed. The arrow in his shoulder hadn't done any permanent damage, but it had done enough. With his breath coming in ragged spasms caused by the intense pain, he fell back into bed.

His mind raced wildly, trying to remember what had done this to him. It had been a beautiful morning when he and Runs with the Wind had ridden into the high mountain meadow. The sun was shining and the early spring, accompanied by exceptionally warm temperatures had already produced the look of summer. Night Hawk, the Cheyenne medicine man, had assured him that it was to early in the season and that cold weather would return for a while longer, but he had felt the need to be home.

As they entered the valley that his family now called home, they saw Spotted Horse sitting astride his huge pinto out in the middle of the meadow. He swung his horse around to face them, and his heart had leaped into his throat when he recognized his sister, sitting in front of the renegade.

The fighting started without any words being exchanged. There was no need for talking. Each man knew it was kill or die. His first shot had been well placed though a little high.

After that all he could remember was trying to work the lever action of his rifle, and his whole world exploding in tremendous pain.

"You're alright," Cheryl said, coming to sit on the edge of her son's bed.

"How did I get here?"

"Run's with the Wind brought you."

"And Misty?"

"No, he went after her when he left here."

"I've got to go with him," Jeremy said trying to get out of bed.

"Lie still," Cheryl said, gently pushing him back down into the covers. "He's been gone for several hours. I sent Mr. Roberts to get Night Hawk, and your pa should be back from the trading post any time now. They'll find Misty, and deal with Spotted Horse."

Cheryl forced a small smile to form on her lips belying the way she felt. If only she could feel as confident as she was trying to make Jeremy think, she might not have the knots in her stomach that threatened to expel it's contents almost constantly.

The evening hours passed slowly into darkness. Jeremy slept fitfully, waking every little bit in a cold sweat from a dream about the plight of his sister. Cheryl passed the hours trying to find solace in the reading of her well worn Bible.

A knock at the door startled Cheryl out of a fitful sleep. Still in her chair by Jeremy's bed where she had been reading her Bible, exhaustion had finally taken it's toll and she had nodded off to sleep.

"Who's There?"

"It's Bob, Ma'm."

"Come in, did you find Night Hawk?" Cheryl didn't wait for him to open the door before assaulting him with questions.

"He's here, so is Antelope, Little Wolf, and a half dozen others."

"Bring them in."

"They are in the barn trying to keep dry until daylight, then they can pick up the trail."

Cheryl noticed then that Mr. Roberts clothes were wet and the faint sound of rain was coming from the roof.

"Get over by the fire and get warm, I'll put some coffee

on."

"If this rain doesn't get any harder or last too long, we should be able to pick up their tracks in a couple more hours."

"Do you think...," her words were interrupted by a light tapping at the door.

"Who is it?"

"Night Hawk, I would see to my son now."

"Come in," Cheryl said swinging the door open for him, "He is over there."

Night Hawk went to the bed where Jeremy was sleeping, and with a touch so soft that it would not disturb the wounded boy, he removed the bandages to inspect the wound. It was well cleaned and showed only a slight redness around the edges. Night Hawk leaned close to smell the wound. Even though the wound was several hours old, it did not have the slightest odor that would indicate the onset of infection.

From inside his shirt, Night Hawk produced a small pouch containing a salve that he had made back at the village while Bob had been giving him the details of the day's events. The wound seemed to be healing well enough on it's own, but Night Hawk applied the salve before rebandaging as a precaution against later infection.

"It is good, he will live. Now we must go find my other son."

"I'm going with you," Bob said as he sat down his nearly empty coffee cup and reached for his slicker that was drying by the fire.

Night Hawk opened the door and stopped in his tracks. The temperature had been slowly dropping all night and the drizzling rain had turned into a lightly falling snow. It hadn't started to stick to the ground yet, but it would only take a few more degrees drop in the temperature and the trail would be lost.

"We must hurry if we are to find the way they went."

Night Hawk stepped to the greying light of predawn and began shouting orders in Cheyenne. Little Wolf and the others came out of the barn leading their horses toward the house. Night Hawk met them halfway and swung to his pony's back. He led the way to the meadow at the far end of the valley where Misty had first been attacked. Bob got his horse out of the barn and followed at a lope.

By the time they reached the meadow the snow was

falling much harder. They stopped to consider the direction that Spotted Horse would take to make his escape.

"He would not go toward the rising sun," Little Wolf said, voicing an opinion everyone shared, "He knows that he is now an enemy of the People."

"If he went north or south," Antelope put in , "he might run into another village of our people, and word would be brought back to us. I think he must have gone into the setting sun."

With a simple command from Night Hawk, the warriors spread out and started working their way toward the west.

Spread out at fifty pace intervals and leading their horses, the warriors worked a zig zag pattern to the west leaving no area unsearched. It was a good effort, but with the snow sticking to the ground now, even the best of trackers would find it an impossible task.

Little Wolf was so involved in trying to discern the meaning of a plant with a broken stem that he didn't see Renegade until the horse was almost to him. He turned to alert the others, and saw that they were already coming his way. Ignoring the horse he squatted back down to study the stem of the broken plant he had found, trying to cover the fact that he had been the last to notice Renegade's approach. Brushing away the snow, he found what he had desperately wanted to find. A small red stain on the green stem could be only one thing, blood.

"One of them is wounded," Little Wolf said as his companions drew near.

"Are you sure?" Antelope asked, questioning the tracking ability of the youth without directly insulting him.

"Yes, Runs with the Wind was not hurt, and there is blood in the trail. Here," he said pointing to the broken stem.

As he looked back down at the stem, he was amazed to see that once again the blood was hidden by snow. He brushed it away and pointed triumphantly at the tiny spot that proved he was right.

"It does not matter," Night Hawk said pushing past the broken stem without a glance. "We will back track Renegade to my son, but we must move quickly for even now his tracks are being covered with snow.

Chapter Twenty Six

Nearly four hours had passed as Misty fed sticks into the fire, before Runs with the Wind came back down the trail. He walked stiff legged through the falling snow with his arms folded tightly across his chest to keep in as much body heat as possible.

She could hear his teeth chattering several steps before he reached the small fire. Misty jumped up and wrapped the small Buffalo robe around his shoulders and helped him to sit under the rock overhang near the fire.

Runs with the Wind sat cross legged, staring across the fire into the darkness. His teeth were clenched to quiet the chattering but he still shivered uncontrollably. Too much body heat had already been lost for him to think rationally, or he would have taken off the sopping wet buckskin pants and sat wrapped only in the buffalo skin allowing the fire to dry and warm his body.

Misty fed more sticks to the fire, in an attempt to get him warm. Steam began to rise from the legs of his pants and still he shook uncontrollably.

"Are you getting any warmer?" she asked.

There was no response other than the constant shivering and ragged breathing that told of a severe cold coming on.

She leaned closer and reached out a hand to break the

trance he seemed to be in. As her fingers touched his leg pain shot through her hand before she could jerk it back. The wet buckskins had been to hot for her to touch and yet he didn't seem to notice. Frantically she jumped to her feet.

"Runs with the Wind," she yelled, "move back from the fire."

Runs with the Wind didn't move. She grabbed the buffalo robe around his shoulders and pulled,. he responded by jerking it out of her hands and pulling it tighter around his shoulders.

Misty grabbed the buffalo robe again and pulled backward with all of her strength as she yelled once again, "Runs with the Wind, you have to move away from the fire."

Tumbling backwards, he scrambled to his feet. Now standing with his back to the fire, he clung to the robe around his shoulders and glared at Misty.

"I'm just trying to help, can't you understand that?"

Still, he only stared into the darkness. Misty realized that he was staring past her, through her, at nothing, just staring. She moved to the side, yet his eyes did not follow. She stepped between him and the fire, and still he gave no indication that she was there.

She touched his wet buckskins on the back of his legs and unlike the front they were icy cold.

"Well, the fire will warm them soon enough," she said it as though he were actually listening.

She tested the front of his pants to see if they were cooling off. To her surprise, they were not only cooling, they were already cold.

"How can I keep you warm if these wet buckskins get cold faster than they get warm?"

She tried turning him as she would a piece of meat on a spit, but it took all of her strength because he wouldn't help. She would have to knock him off balance and try to force him into the desired position as he struggled to regain his footing.

Her exerted energy was keeping her warm enough that she didn't realize that her fire was dying down. She had to find a way to keep Runs with the Wind moving and take care of the fire at the same time.

She knelt down to put a few more sticks on the fire and noticed how warm the air was at the back of the depression in the rock. She felt the stone surface. The fire had not only broken the chill of it, but had actually warmed it considerably. She also noticed the ground close to the fire was warmer.

Struck by a sudden inspiration, she used one of the larger sticks to scrape the bed of coals about three feet farther away from the rocks. She added more wood and in seconds had it going nicely again. She scraped away the remaining coals, and threw several handfuls of the warm dry dirt over the old fire pit. Now all she had to do was to get Runs with the Wind to sit in this warmer location and keep a low constant fire going.

She went to his side and tried gently coaxing him toward the fire. He wouldn't budge. She felt the wet buckskins again. They were colder than ever, and his shivering was getting worse. She stepped around to the far side of him and shoved with all her might. He stumbled in the right direction, and before he could catch his balance, she shoved him again. Now he was within two steps of where she wanted him, but because the rock overhang was too low for him to walk under, the tripping technique would no longer work.

She tested the ground where she wanted him to sit. Still hot but she had no choice, she couldn't let him just stand there and freeze.

Now came the hard part. She had to get him to get out of his wet pants. They were sucking the heat out of him faster than his body could make it.

"Take off your pants," she said as firmly as she could.

Again there was no response.

"I said take off your pants!"

Still shivering violently, Runs with the Wind stood staring into the cold night air.

"Oh Runs with the Wind, what would you do if it were me freezing to death?"

Without waiting for the response she knew wasn't coming, she answered her own question.

"I know, you'd have me sitting next to a nice warm fire with nothing on but that buffalo robe, and have my clothes hanging up to dry, and the whole time you would be a gentleman and pretend not to notice. I hope I can do the same for you."

Without another word or thought about it, she set to removing his moccasins and then his buckskin pants. Again she tested the spot where the fire had been and it was still almost to hot for bare skin, but she had no choice. She wrapped the buffalo robe around his shoulders and shoved him to the ground. He seemed not to notice that anything had changed as he sat there shivering. Misty hung his buckskins on a bush that was just close enough to the fire to eventually get them dry and then set herself back to the task of taking care of her patient.

The feel of his skin was cold and clammy, like something long dead. She put more wood on the fire and sat down next to him. She pulled the robe tight around both of them and wrapped an arm around his shoulders trying to give him some of the warmth from her own body. He showed no sign that he even knew that she was there, so she held the robe around them with one hand and with the other she fed sticks into the small fire upon which their lives depended. Occasionally she would climb out of the robe to gather more sticks for the fire and to turn his buckskins around so that both sides would dry.

After a while she noticed that he had slumped forward in sleep, and though he no longer shivered and didn't feel quite so cold to the touch, his breathing was still very raspy.

She too was getting sleepy, and she fought to stay awake, to feed wood into the fire. Their lives depended on it.

Chapter Twenty Seven

Antelope raced ahead to catch Renegade who welcomed the approach of the familiar scent. One quick glance revealed the wound that had sent the horse running in panic.

"Little Wolf, take him home and care for the wound," Antelope said, holding the reins out toward him.

"I can't leave now, I have to help find Runs with the Wind."

"Now you have to take care of the horse. There are plenty of us to look for Runs with the Wind, and we need someone who can find Jeremy's cabin in this storm."

Little Wolf had no desire to leave the search party, but it was a huge boost to his pride that he alone had been deemed worthy and capable to handle the task at hand. With his head held high, Little Wolf took the reins of the exhausted horse and turned back along the trail toward Jeremy's cabin.

Night Hawk and Antelope led the way, as the search party followed Renegade's tracks back toward whatever had become of Runs with the Wind. They moved fast, as the now heavy falling snow blanketed everything.

"We must move quickly," Night Hawk said as he watched the snow sticking to the freshly made hoof prints. "The tracks will soon be gone."

The light of dawn did nothing to help find the tracks that soon vanished beneath a sea of white. Renegade's frightened escape had taken him far to the south before he had calmed down enough to turn toward home. He had only come back to the trail at the spot where they had found him because of the sound and smell of other horses.

The trail they had followed led them over rough broken ground. Clearly the horse had been unsure of the way home and might have been lost in the storm completely had it not heard the approach of the search party. Back and forth the trail wound through the brush until it was totally lost beneath the new snow.

"It is of no use to follow this trail any further," Night Hawk announced stopping in the middle of the trail. "The snow has completely hidden the tracks, and Renegade was not following any trail."

"The storm is letting up," Antelope interjected, hoping that this information would somehow make Night Hawk feel a little better about the situation.

"It will not matter, the tracks will still be hidden for many days."

Slowly, and without a word, the rest of the search party turned their ponies back toward the cabin, and followed Night Hawk in silence.

Nature had beaten them once again, and none among the searchers had any hope of finding Runs With the Wind, or the Little Sun Spirit.

Little Wolf, however, with the enthusiasm of youth, had no intentions of giving up. Since he had taken Jeremy's horse home, the rest of the search party was already a long ways ahead of him, and trying to catch up was not his idea of a daring rescue.

"I'm going after them," he announced to Cheryl as he turned to leave the cabin.

"I'm going with you," Josh said, leaping to his feet. Since the time he had been rescued from his grandfather's evil beatings, he had become more and more fond of the family that had saved him. Especially Misty, and if Little Wolf thought there was a chance of finding her, he was going to do everything he could to help.

"No Josh," Cheryl said as she stepped in front of the door to block his path. "You don't know the country to the west, and I don't want you lost out there too."

"I'll be fine as long as I stay with Little Wolf, besides your family saved my life not to long ago, and I can't sit here doing nothing while Misty is in danger."

He stepped around Cheryl and was out the door before she had a chance to respond. Not that she had a good argument, but even though she was proud of the kind of man he was growing into, it was hard to let a boy of not quite fifteen go out into a frozen wilderness for any reason.

"Wait up Little Wolf," Josh said running for the barn.

His horse still stood where he had left it, with the saddle resting lightly on his back. In seconds he had the cinch tightened and was following Little Wolf at a dead run down the valley.

By the time they came to the place where he had last seen the trail, all sign of any passage had been covered by two or three inches of soft powdery snow. The boys looked toward the western horizon searching out the most likely trails for Spotted Horse to make his escape. Occasionally you could see a narrow ribbon of white that told of a trail beneath. With no weeds or grass growing in the paths, they were easier to see at long distance with snow on the ground. Now the only question was which trail to follow.

"We'll just have to try each one until we find something," Little Wolf said.

"Which one first?"

"The last sign I saw was headed straight west, I say we take that one first."

They had ridden several hundred yards along the trail without finding any sign before stopping.

"I think we should try another trail," Josh said swinging his horse around to head back.

"It's hard to know for sure..."

Little Wolf was interrupted by the sound of a bleating, buffalo calf.

"What?"

"The buffalo, did you not hear it?"

"So what?"

"Look closely. See the beaded leather strap around his neck. It is the Spirit Buffalo that helped Jeremy and Runs with the Wind during the first snows."

"What are you talking about?"

"It's a long story, Runs With the Wind can tell you after we find him. Now we must follow the calf without disturbing him."

"I don't see what good it's going to do to follow a buffalo calf around the woods when we should be trying to find them instead."

"The calf will find them for us. He thinks Jeremy is his mother, and identifies Renegade's scent with Jeremy."

"What do you mean, he thinks Jeremy is his mother?"

"I told you, it's a long story, and it does not matter now, what matters is that he can follow Renegades scent even with the trail covered with snow."

"How?"

"Buffalo have good noses for finding little bunches of grass under a lot more snow than this. To follow a living scent he just brushes the snow aside with his nose and smells the ground."

Before long the buffalo calf shied away from a lump in the snow and continued along the trail. The conspicuous lump was only a few feet from the trail, but it was far enough not to disturb the calf too bad.

Not really wanting to, Little Wolf eased forward to inspect the lump. Gently brushing back the snow he uncovered the body of Red Fox.

"That helps," he said looking up at Josh, "at least there are only two of them for Runs with the Wind to deal with."

Chapter Twenty Eight

The snow was still falling as the eastern sky began to lighten. Misty fed more sticks into the fire, and felt Runs with the Wind stir as she moved away from him. His skin no longer felt cold and clammy to the touch, in fact he felt quite warm. She checked his forehead, as her mother had checked her's so many times before. He was too warm now and had a fever but she must first concentrate on finding some food.

She slipped out of the robe and stood next to the fire rubbing her legs to get the circulation back, and then helped Runs with the Wind into a comfortable sitting position in front of the fire. He snuggled deeper into the buffalo robe and closed his eyes.

"Wake up," Misty said shaking him by the shoulder.

"Let me sleep."

"You have to get dressed first. Then you can sleep all you want," Misty said holding his buckskins close to the fire to warm them.

"Later, now I just want to sleep."

"Now," she said shoving his buckskins into his hand, and reaching for his moccasins.

Realizing that it would take more energy to resist than it would to comply, Runs with the Wind began to dress. Once he had his pants and moccasins on, and was again wrapped in the buffalo robe, he admitted, if only to himself, that he did feel much better.

"Keep the fire going, I'll look around for something to eat."

He didn't have much hope of her coming back with anything, but he was used to missing several meals at a time on hunting trips or occasions when time did not allow searching for food.

"Don't go to far," he cautioned as Misty walked out of their makeshift camp.

"I won't be too long."

She started working her way back along the trail they had followed the night before. She stopped often to look at various plants, but could find nothing that she was familiar with as edible. She nearly jumped out of her skin when a small snow shoe rabbit leaped out of the brush at her feet.

The rabbit was young and inexperienced with human predators, and ran only a short distance before stopping to sit very still in another clump of brush. Blending into his surroundings was one of his best defenses, but he didn't count on someone who could see that the tracks in the fresh snow led right to his hiding spot.

Not totally unfamiliar with the art of hunting, Misty eased forward, stepping lightly so as not to spook the young rabbit. Each step she took found her looking, not for the rabbit because she knew where he was, but for some kind of weapon to use on him.

Just a few steps short of the prey, she found what she was looking for. It was a stout stick, eighteen inches long and as big around as her wrist. She pulled, gently easing it out of the undergrowth, trying not to alert her quarry. Two more steps and she would be in striking range. She eased back the stick and took another step forward. Snap! The little twig buried beneath the snow sounded like a rifle shot in the crisp morning air.

The rabbit didn't wait around to see what had made the noise. Darting quickly through the brush he found another hiding spot. Undaunted by the mishap, Misty continued along the trail determined to be even more quiet. Once again as she neared striking range, the young rabbit darted away.

"Darn rabbit!" Misty yelled as she threw her club at the fleeing snow shoe.

To her surprise, as much as that of the rabbit, the stick found it's mark. Squealing in pain, from several broken ribs and a broken leg bone, the rabbit tried to escape. Like a starving animal, her survival instincts kicked in and Misty snatched up the stick to pursue the rabbit relentlessly.

Crashing through the brush, she swung her club viciously at everything in her path. Twigs and leaves flew through the air as she struggled through the thick undergrowth. Closer and closer she came with each attack, until the snowshoe ran out of places to hide. He made one last valiant effort to escape by attempting to cross a narrow clearing that stood between him and the safety of the heavy growth of brush along the creek.

It was a good try, but Misty was to fast for him. She dove into the clearing, bringing the club down on his head as she landed outstretched, face down on the snow covered ground. Scrambling to her knees, she clubbed the rabbit until there was no longer any movement. With a sigh of relief, she gathered up her prize and headed back to camp.

Runs with the Wind sat up next to the fire as Misty proudly walked into camp with her fresh kill. She dropped it at his feet and squatted next to the fire to warm her nearly frozen hands.

He made no mention of the blood that nearly covered her hands and face, or of the scratches she had gotten from the brush, that was causing the blood to flow so freely. From the looks of her it had been pretty much a fair fight, and the fact that they were going to eat at all, was do to her efforts alone.

"It is good," he said barely able to keep a straight face as he examined what was left of the rabbit.

"I hope so. It wasn't easy getting a rabbit with a stick."

"I don't think it was easy on the rabbit either," Runs with the Wind snickered under his breath, and Misty taught him another custom of the white man, as she hit him in the back of the head with a snowball.

"Next time you go find breakfast, and I'll sit next to a nice warm fire."

For a split second she had been mad at him for making fun of the condition her rabbit was in, but even if it had not been beaten ridiculously bad, it would have been impossible for her to stay mad. One of the things she liked about him was his ability to find humor in almost any situation.

Within a few minutes the rabbit was cooking over a nice hot bed of coals. It wasn't going to be a feast by any means, but right now it smelled as tantalizing as anything Misty had ever eaten. Jeremy had been right when he said there was nothing like missing a few meals in a row to make you appreciate even the simplest of meals.

It was nearly noon by the time they started down the trail for home. Runs with the Wind still didn't feel very much like traveling, but every step he took, put them one step closer to home. He couldn't believe how sore he felt. Every muscle in his body ached. It must have been caused by the tremendous amount of shivering he had done as his body tried to fight off the effects of hypothermia. Whatever the cause, each step seemed more painful than the last and their progress became less and less with each passing hour.

Chapter Twenty Nine

Throughout the morning, Little Wolf and Josh followed the young buffalo. They were making good progress when the buffalo calf stopped to wander back and forth in a small clearing before continuing on his way. As he passed out of sight, Little Wolf climbed down from his horse to examine the ground where the calf had spent so much time.

"He stopped here for a while, something must have happened."

Just then the buffalo calf snorted, and jumped away from a lump in the snow that seem to bear a great resemblance to the one that had hidden the body of Red Fox. Slowly, he worked his way around the obstruction in the trail and continued on. Little Wolf let him move on down the trail for some distance before going to investigate what had spooked the calf.

Easing closer to the lump in the snow Little Wolf took his time. Whatever it was, Little Wolf was in no hurry to look, and it would be no problem for them to catch up to the calf later. Seeing no movement or tracks other than those of the buffalo, Little Wolf stepped closer to the lump and brushed away some of the snow.

Little Wolf felt a knot in his stomach as he realized that what he had found was another body. Slowly, almost afraid to look for fear of what he might find, he brushed away more snow until he could identify the unfortunate man in the snow.

"Coyote Track," he whispered in relief.

"What is it?" Josh asked.

"Coyote Track," Little Wolf answered. "That evens the odds a little more, now all that is left for him to deal with is Spotted Horse."

Climbing back on his horse, Little Wolf started on down the trail left by the buffalo. A few minutes later, he was once again in sight. Now however he was milling around, going back and forth as though he were confused. Slowly but surely he continued to move along the trail and the boys were able to get close enough to see what had confused him.

"Tracks in the snow," Little Wolf said.

"What kind of tracks?"

"They were made by the white mans shoes, but very small."

"That would have to be Misty. She must be alright."

"There is blood along the trail. Not much, but she may be hurt."

"We've got to find her, it'll be dark before too much longer."

"We don't have to wait for the buffalo calf any more, we should be able to find her from the tracks she is leaving. If the calf follows Runs with the Wind in another direction, we can pick up the trail later."

They skirted around the buffalo and picked up the tracks a little farther down the trail. Taking off at a lope they raced along the path easily following the clearly marked trail in the long shadows of late afternoon. Within minutes the buffalo calf was racing along behind, not wanting to be left alone again.

Before long they reached the temporary campsite and wasted no time trying to figure out the condition of their friends. It was clear, by the two sets of tracks, that they were together. They still didn't know the whereabouts of Spotted Horse, but the afternoon light was beginning to fade, and they quickly decided they would continue to follow as fast as possible, and deal with Spotted Horse, when and if they came across him.

It was nearly dark when they spotted the two exhausted travelers trudging through the snow. Shouting and waving their arms, they raced along no longer needing to follow a trail.

Sliding his horse to a stop, Little Wolf bailed off to greet his friend. "I knew you would be alright," he said clasping a hand on Runs with the Wind's shoulder.

"Did you bring food?"

"Food? No thanks for finding us, just where is the food?" Josh was astounded.

"We're not lost, just tired and hungry," Runs with the Wind replied, trying to keep a straight face.

"But..."

Josh's words were suddenly cut short by the sound of laughter, not only from Runs with the Wind, but from Little Wolf and Misty who also understood his strange sense of humor.

After the laughter subsided, Little Wolf was the first to speak. "Do you want to make camp for the night, or just keep going?"

"I think we should keep going," Misty said, "I just want to get home to my own bed."

Little Wolf handed the reins of his horse to Runs with the Wind, who looked like he had walked about as far as he was going to on this night. Thanking his friend he swung onto the back of the young stallion and extended a hand toward Misty. Gratefully she took his hand and climbed on behind him.

"No sense walking," Josh said reaching down to Little Wolf, "mine rides double too."

Through most of the night they headed east, letting the horses take their time under the increased load. Josh couldn't help but feel a twinge of jealousy as he watched Misty snuggle up close to Runs with the Wind and doze peacefully as they rode along. He had assumed that since he was the only white boy for more than a hundred miles in any direction, that someday he and Misty would be married. To see her taking to Runs with the Wind.... well it just wasn't right.

The rest of the search party had picked up their trail after giving up on backtracking Renegade, and caught up to them just before they reached the valley that Misty's family called home. As they made their way up to the cabin the sun was just beginning it's daily run across the sky. John had also returned to the valley from his trip to the trading post, and helped Jeremy out onto the porch to welcome his sister and brother home.

"Are they....," he asked hesitantly.

"They won't bother anyone again."

"Let's get you into the house," Cheryl said helping Misty down from her horse. "You too Runs with the Wind, I'll have a nice hot breakfast for all of you in no time at all."

"Where did he come from?" Jeremy asked noticing the buffalo calf for the first time.

"That's how they found us, he was following the scent of your horse looking for his mother. I think you should at least say hello."

"I'll do more than that. Nothing but the best for my spirit animal. Come on boy, lets see if we can find you a nice warm spot in the barn and a big bucket of oats."

"What do you mean spirit animal?" John asked, as he stepped off of the porch with Jeremy, "and what are we going to do with a buffalo?"

"Make a lot of Cheyenne people very happy," Night Hawk said through his laughter, remembering all of the havoc the calf had created in the winter camp. "I think he is going to like it here."

SNEAK PREVIEW OF BOOK THREE

ZEB'S REVENGE

Chapter One

Zeb shivered slightly against the cold morning air as he fed a few more small sticks into the campfire that he had become so accustomed to. It was nearly spring, but even this late snow couldn't do anything to dampen his spirits. For the best part of a year he had been camping on the trail, trying to track down the people who had taken away his oldest son at gun point. By the time he had recovered from the bullet wound in his shoulder, that he had received from Jimmy the scout for the wagon train, it had become apparent that his brother Jed would not be coming back with the boy. Most likely Jimmy had been waiting for Jed to come, and had set a trap. Though he hadn't taken time to dig up either of the graves along the trail of the wagon train, Zeb knew now that his brother was in the bottom of one of them.

That was another score he had to settle with these folks that had disrupted their lives so badly. He had chased the wagon train all the way to Oregon before catching them, only to find that John's family, and the family that now had Josh, had left the wagon train in Colorado territory. It had been a long trip back, but that was alright too, because it put him closer to the young Indian boy, Runs with the Wind, who was responsible for his brother's death.

He grimaced in pain as he stretched to put a few more sticks on the fire, and cursed Mr. Reeves like he did every morning since they had met up in Oregon. It had been his intent to beat the information he wanted out of the smaller man, but as it turned out he was fortunate to get away with his life. Mr. Reeves wasn't as big as Zeb, but he was surprisingly fast with his fists, and every punch thrown seemed to do more damage than the one before. Under the circumstances Zeb felt lucky to have gotten away with a broken nose and a few broken ribs, some of which had not been set straight before healing. It was those ribs that brought the pain, and the constant reminder of the beating he had gotten that day.

If it hadn't been for the young lady who helped the doctor patch him up, he might still be trying to find out the information he needed. Fortunately she had been more than willing to answer his questions, thinking that he was trying to find some long lost relatives. Had she known what he was planning for the young boy and the people who had rescued him from the plight in the first place, she would not have been so free with her information.

"Someday, Mr. Reeves, someday," Zeb spoke between clenched teeth, thinking that it was just one more score that needed taking care of, "but right now I have more pressin' matters to tend to."

Some time during the night, the snow had stopped, and the sky was beginning to clear as the sun rose over the plains to the east. Zeb knew he was close to the place where John and the others had left the wagon train, and all he had to do was head north toward the highest peak visible from where he now sat. Somewhere, in a valley below that peak, his search would end.

No longer in a hurry, he sipped a second cup of steaming hot coffee while he tried to formulate some sort of plan. This was not going to be a simple matter of grabbing his son and racing back across the plains, there was a matter of revenge to be taken on those who had wronged his family.

"Yea John, I'll learn ya not to be mixin' in the private affairs of the Harrison family, I just ain't figured out how I'll go about it yet, but I will. You can count on it."

The evil grin he had inherited from his father once again came to his lips as he threw the grounds of his coffee into the fire and began to break camp. His horse stood patiently as Zeb cinched up the saddle, but as he roughly forced the bit into the horses mouth, it startled him, making him jerk his head up and away. This in turn jerked hard on Zeb's arm, that was holding the bridle, causing a sharp pain in his ribs. Zeb picked up a broken limb from the ground and swatted the horse across the face. With his front feet still hobbled the horse couldn't get away from his attacker, and took several more sharp blows as he tried. Finally, terrified and shaking the horse submitted, and stood with his head down shaking in fear of what might follow.

"That's better," Zeb said to the subdued animal,"you'd

BOOK ORDER FORM

Please send me the following books:

	Qty.	Price	Total
Runs with the Wind	____	$6.95	____
Spirit of the Buffalo	____	$6.95	____
Coming soon Zeb's Revenge			

For products shipped to Arizona please
add 7.7%=$0.54 cents sales tax per book   ____

Shipping and Handling
$2.50 for first book
and $1.00 for each additional book
Contact Publisher for International shipping rates

<u>For orders of 10 or more please contact publisher</u>

BOOK ORDER TOTAL   ____

Please ship books to (your address):

Name _____

Address _____

City, State, Zip _____

Renegade Publishing
P.O. Box 544
Camp Verde, AZ 86322
books@RenegadePublishing.com

BOOK ORDER FORM

Please send me the following books:

	Qty.	Price	Total
Runs with the Wind	————	$6.95	————
Spirit of the Buffalo	————	$6.95	————
Coming soon Zeb's Revenge			

For products shipped to Arizona please
add 7.7%=$0.54 cents sales tax per book   ————

Shipping and Handling
$2.50 for first book
and $1.00 for each additional book
Contact Publisher for International shipping rates

For orders of 10 or more please contact publisher

BOOK ORDER TOTAL   ————

Please ship books to (your address):

Name   _____

Address   _____

City, State, Zip   _____

Renegade Publishing
P.O. Box 544
Camp Verde, AZ 86322
books@RenegadePublishing.com